I0571753

POWERHOUSE

RACE

A WRIGHT SERIES

Book 5

Linda McKown

POWERHOUSE RACE

ISBN-13: 978-0-9997357-4-9

Author:
LindaMcKownAuthor LLC
11574 E Running Deer Trail
Scottsdale, AZ 85262
http://www.lindamckown.com

Any names of people and entities are fictitious in this story having been created by the author's imagination.

Front Cover Photo of the book is copyright through Shutterstock. Book title manipulation was done by Joseph McKown

Dedicated to my fan readers, race car drivers, and to my family who sees my need to write and share stories. Also, to my dad and brothers: Raymond, Roger, and Gary because they loved all kinds of cars.

See the back page for a list of my other books.

Contents

1   Meeting with a Driver

JIM MICHAELS AND Tami Cortez went to meet with the race car driver, Mic Palla, at the race track in Michigan. They were part of Derek's team. Derek Wright, the Los Angeles investigator, was busy checking out newly-found information regarding the Snake woman poisoner and her deserted island property. Rhonda Peters, another investigator in his office was flying with Derek to Shannen Island in the Caribbean. They were helping the police investigate the Snake woman case. They hoped to find clues at one of her former locations.

Jim and Tami were undercover agents sent to protect Mic and help with the investigation about a milder poisoning hit done to a race car driver. The poison was the same type used by Snake woman. They weren't sure the Snake woman did this mild a hit because of another case in Miami. Therein, lied the mystery to the poisoning.

"Who did what and why? How did the powerhouse racer become someone's target? Was he supposed to die or not? Who were his enemies?"

At the last minute, Tami brought her sister, Tiare, who recently graduated from the police academy in Miami, along to meet with Mic Palla. Derek agreed that Tiare's inside information regarding race car drivers would help.

Tiare dated a Texas race car driver for almost a year named Dan Jaehn who was currently a close competitor driver and was working the same races. The race car drivers' number of wins and racing style matched each other closely on the race car circuit, making them exciting conversation for the media.

Mic was released from the Los Angeles hospital after his close call with death from a dose of African Mamba snake poison and would be racing in the big race in four weeks. His pit crew, team, and cars were ready. The cars still needed to pass final inspections. They moved Mic's luxury motorhome to the Michigan drivers' lot location.

Mic and Dan were talking to their separate pit crews at the track when Jim, Tami, and Tiare arrived. They wore clearance badges to access the race track as very important people, so they could complete some media interviews. Their badges also contained special top security privilege which included the track and pit areas.

At the bottom of the stands, Tiare saw her friend, Dan Jaehn. She let Tami know she would meet them later at Mic's motorhome. She needed to talk to her old friend.

The guard stopped Tiare from entering the pit area. Dan looked up and saw the beautiful young red-haired woman. He noticed her white dress and white hat with red band and four-inch stilettos. Dan waved the guard to let her past the first gate. He headed toward her at a run, picked Tiare up, and twirled her around.

Mic saw the commotion and watched the two sophisticated young people.

"Tiare, you are my darling woman."

She knew he still liked her. She jumped exuberantly in his arms. He held her even tighter as she stilled in his arms. He was delighted.

"All the country stars aren't as bright as you are in your red shoes. In a heartbeat, I would know you at any distance, because you're the only woman I know that can glide that way. Let's not mention the other reason which is that you can swing and stomp to a Texas two-step in stilettos. How are you? Are you here to see me? If so, I'm extremely pleased. This race will be good times again."

"Hi, Tex, I'm just fine. I did stop by to say hello to my favorite friend but am also here doing some tag-a-long work for my sister which is mainly background research on some of the drivers. Therefore, you will see me on occasion doing interviews. My sister wants to do a magazine article on the thrill of racing. That is why we have the special media badges."

He took off her hat and kissed her full on the mouth smearing her lipstick a little. Taking out his handkerchief, she helped him wipe it off his face and lips. He kept his arm around her.

"You are the only person whom I will allow to call me Tex and you know it. You must use my real name if you're sticking around to admire me in the race with the rest of the spectators. I don't need another tag to my name. Do you require any better tickets? I can get you great seats for future races. How about we go eat dinner this evening?"

"I already made my arrangement for tickets, but thanks anyway. Yes, dinner will be fun. I am hungry for conversation and food. Pick me up at seven at the Canter Hotel. I'll wait outside with the doorman. But now, I must attend a meeting. You will see me this evening. Oh, and I want a steak dinner with salad plus real expensive red wine. No cheeseburgers and root beer for dinner this time."

"I know the perfect place" said Dan. "See, I remember you like steak and I'm always a fast learner."

Tex reluctantly let go of her. Mic, Jim, and Tami left the pit area and walked to the motorhome lot.

XXXXXX

Tiare went to the ladies' room to repair her lipstick. She was here to help her sister out. Having walked through the back gate to the reserved-for-drivers-only section of the motorhome lot, she saw the large haulers for the race cars.

Mic's sleek black motorhome was in its slot and looked identical to her police file photos. There were bright yellow wheel tracks on the side with his last name "PALLA" in slightly blurred red letters to indicate speed.

This meeting with the super driver should be interesting were her thoughts as she approached the motorhome door. She adjusted her white wide brimmed hat and knocked on the metal frame. She was looking at the bottom of the door, expecting his security people to let her in.

She looked up to see Mic's dark hazel eyes and medium brown hair looking directly into her gold brown eyes. He saw a sprinkling of freckles that she must have hated. The freckles, he could clearly see, she tried to hide with makeup on her nose, and he noticed the poppy-red lipstick on her full lips. He thought of the phantom red race car. Everything red that she wore started his engine. Mic noticed her tiny waist. He took her hand and helped her up the step, moving her very close to his tall muscled and finely-tuned frame.

"You must be the third powerful wonder woman who is undercover with the police. Rhonda is a doll and very married. I just learned from your beautiful sister, Tami Cortez, that you are Tiare Cruz. You have come to rescue me. I like your name by the way. Isn't your first name some gardenia flower found in Tahiti or the awesome South Pacific?"

Tiare was interested in a man who knew about flowers. This was something new to her. She knew immediately who the handsome man was in front of her. She thought of him as super, confident, stud-factor, heavily-experienced male. Rhonda had told her to proceed with caution with this race car driver. She was familiar with the type and unafraid to enter the heat.

"Yes, my name is Tiare Cruz and you are Mic Palla. The name on your wonder throne is visible. Or should we call it coach? I'm surprised you know the flower. You must have traveled to the famous islands frequently. You don't look like you need rescuing for the moment. I was told you are a powerhouse in a race and an evil poisoner's personal toy. I'm sorry about the poison part. No one needs that in their life."

Mic smiled. He more than liked her first name. Her name was unusual like her. He also knew it closely matched the word tiara. She was impressed with his name on the motorhome. He did acknowledge that his rig was impressive. It was worth every penny if either his motorhome or his charisma caught her attention. She looked like a fun person. He was bored with the track girls that flocked around his race car. This girl had substance, not to mention class. He loved class. His last five wives were classy until they left him.

He could just see his lawyer shaking his head at the speed with which he connected with women. Mic didn't care. Money was secondary. Magic was standing in front of him. Racing and women were number one. The order flipped with the breeze. It was a love-love relationship. His lawyer only saw the love-hate stuff. Mic knew there was more. He wouldn't miss a heartbeat in the love-capture zone. He noted that she was worried about his welfare. Caring was a good sign.

"I've been to Bora Bora a couple times on my honeymoons, which I'm sure those pieces of information are in your files. But I prefer the island of Moorea instead. Its beauty and heart shape pull a person into mystery and excitement. I like the original name of the island which is Aimeo. I do need rescuing all the time. Plus, I know that I'm a powerhouse in a race and elsewhere. I'm very good at a lot of things as you will certainly find out."

"Ah, yes, perhaps Aimeo is the mysterious magical place like the island someone named Bali Hai."

Tiare was staying away from the other things he was good at.

Then he stepped back to let her pass, smelling her sweet fragrant cologne, which did have a hint of gardenia and watched her silky auburn red hair swing. Her hair reminded him of liquid brandy in a crystal decanter. The swirl with brandy was part of the flavor enhancement. Mic knew this investigation was going to ramp up. He saw only an open track with illuminated green lights and a checkered flag at the very end.

Mic grinned. He loved stilettos and all gorgeous-figured women. This Tiare person had both those going for her. She would be more than one of the perks of his job. He hoped she was going to stick around the tracks and not leave after Michigan.

He wanted to take her to a French Polynesian island.

Mic responded, "Yes, definitely Bali Hai." While thinking to himself, he would have included at the end of the sentence, "and the Tiare flower."

He didn't know her or what else she did for fun, but he would immediately find out. She was from Miami and those women enjoyed fun. He worried because Miami was overflowing with wannabe jocks and rich millionaires. She probably knew some of those men. That meant experienced, plus she was a cop. His game would need to be better.

Mic was thinking dinner this evening would be excellent. He was good at manipulation and games. The race car track was always a new one to work his skills. Mic figured Dan already asked her out on a date, and he would have one of his security men cancel that one. He would collect this gorgeous woman at her hotel, drive his sports car to a nice restaurant, and take her to dinner.

He knew Dan would be more than pissed when he found out later about the botched dinner with a friend. He could handle Dan. Tiare may also be upset. The red hair worried him a little bit. *He wasn't sure he could handle her.*

If the media saw them, it would be a circus. Their pictures would be in the paper. The paper would fuel Dan's competitive hatred even more toward him. Mic thought about it a moment and smiled. He didn't care about Dan. "Bumped off the track again. I know you hate to lose your slot. That's why they call it a race."

Now, love, there was always the beginning part. In a race, there was the beginning to every piece in the chain. Who didn't want the beginning part? Revving engines, squealing tires, and smoke. Then there was the speed. Afterwards, the win-win part. It was like eating the icing on a cake first and then the wonderful chocolate ganache or strawberry filling at the winner's circle.

New love or new beginnings held tastes that filled one's senses, not to mention charm and mystery. This young woman was worth the trouble. She looked like love extraordinaire and endless possibilities. Mic could see themselves flying down the road flipping over the backroads airborne on occasion when the road dipped. Every curve of her body was committed to memory like each turn in the track. He knew her like he did his well-tuned race car which he handled with expert skill.

His past visions of their encounter hadn't impaired his keen sense of competition. He checked her smooth fingers when he helped her up the step and noticed no rings. When she had kissed Dan, he became intrigued. There was more than his heart racing. He was going to have dinner with her and no one was going to get in his way.

Tiare and the rest of Derek's team left the motorhome. Mic was alone but decided to go back to the pit. Mic stopped himself from singing a song he wrote a long time ago. There was a reason to rewrite the words now that he met Tiare. He whistled the tune instead as he walked past Dan in the bleachers.

Dan frowned, stopped, and watched Mic walking backwards up the steps. Then Dan ran into a little old lady. Dan apologized profusely and signed another autograph on the woman's lace handkerchief. Dan hurried off.

Mic disappeared down the long corridor. Dan figured that Mic was up to something but couldn't figure out what changed today. He was stumped and disturbed.

Mic totally forgot about the poisoner and his near escape from death. All he could see was Dan's face of consternation when Mic peeked around the corner. Mic could feel the lift of excitement. Dan was clueless.

Mic did another little circular dance and walked backwards again. The steps were a perfect imitation of his prior drill. It was a good thing the little old lady hadn't seen Mic. She would have thought all the young drivers at this track were weird and a little looney.

"I feel like a renegade. Rivalry is very rejuvenating, and the night was still young. Both concepts were better to look forward to than any Zen experience. "I wonder if she likes massage," said Mic to the air. His feelings and thoughts flashed. He was already racing the track of new experiences. His past difficulties with women were forgotten.

2   Deserted Island

DEREK WALKED THROUGH the empty house on the island with Rhonda and the realtor. They took the float charter plane over, and the woman realtor hired the cheaper motorboat launch. She was there picking up her electronic lockbox and the extra key. They were informed by the realtor that Shannen Island was sold last week, and the new owners were currently in Japan for two months on vacation. There was no trace of where the furniture, equipment, or money from the sale went.

There was an area which contained several burn barrels, except stirring the ashes produced no recognizable piece of paper. Total nonexistence was the words to describe the former owner and where her assets went.

"Nice pad. The place would be hard to leave. It is an island paradise. I wonder how long the person lived here. It possibly was for some time as the wall paint was an older color," said Rhonda.

"You know wall paint colors? I'm impressed always with the female mind. Could you find out the history of the owners of the island and any people who may have visited or lived here previously? There must be a connection somewhere. This is such an out of the way place, not the usual tourist location. Whoever lived here must have lots of money and be a person who traveled extensively. They were possibly looking for two people, a man and a woman."

"I will get right on the search. If the Snake woman lived in such a nice place, then her next home would be luxurious and well-equipped. I saw the urinal in the second bathroom. There definitely was a man with the woman. Their future home will also be out of the way from tourists, perhaps a small town a reasonable distance away. Some generators just like the ones found here could possibly be used at the new location. I'll contact the manufacturer of the generators to ask for a list of purchases in the last seven years."

"Good idea on the generators and check with the airplane float manufacturers. These people might miss a detail at some point in time. It was good odds that the two people might lean toward the same specific companies' products. The law of averages should start playing against them. Uncloaking their dark shields is what I hope we can accomplish in the future."

Derek touched a diagram on one of the outside walls. It was a set of hashtags. The lines made no sense to him. There were arrows.

There was not a worker or animal around. Only the seagulls at the end of the long boat dock broke the horizon. The island was reclusive and required a trip via a large boat, float plane, or helicopter. Derek figured they must have used float planes, and he placed a search for small airports with landing sites close to water. There were three possible locations within a float plane's flying range.

They flew to each site and eventually found the two sets of extra floats from the woman's airplanes. The two airplanes were not at the site and the owner of the small landing location knew no information regarding the lessors. Derek knew this last site was where they disembarked from this part of the continent. The Snake woman was probably living in another country. Her escape and cover were complete. The woman was highly educated and skilled for a con artist.

3   Dinner with Tiare

TIARE CAME THROUGH the revolving doors of the hotel to see the doorman holding open a sports car door for her. She assumed Dan arrived. The sports car had been waiting over thirty minutes. The driver was unsure of the exact time for the dinner date. She slid into the seat and glanced at the driver. The man was wrong for her date. She was surprised. She tried to exit the vehicle.

Mic held up his hands in surrender. She looked around at the scene. There was no one except them and the doorman. The doorman shrugged his shoulders. She turned back towards the handsomely-dressed man. She said, "Mic, why in the world are you here waiting for me? There must be a mistake. You're not my date."

"No, I'm not your date." He nodded to the door man who quickly fled the scene.

"However, I'm very happy to accommodate the change in plans. Starving for food, I thought you might like a steak dinner tonight. Besides, we didn't have time to really chat this afternoon. Now would be the perfect time seeing as how the other plans are canceled."

"Dan canceled dinner? Why would he cancel our dinner engagement? He must have something important that he forgot." Tiare was disappointed that she couldn't pick up on lost time.

"It probably was one of those sponsor deals going on with the guy that made him forget about such

14

a beautiful woman. Or perhaps that last timed run left the brain impaired.

Tiare still looked doubtful.

"Now I would never forget how great you looked this morning at the track. I know that he saw you but perhaps it was old impact. Now with me, the impact clearly rocked me off the stool that I was sitting on. I know that sounds minor except that I don't usually go there. If my brain slows, I kick it into full speed. My brain also works fine going any speed but moves miraculously at two hundred miles per hour. I'm going there with your beautiful eyes. By the way, you look even better in the evening light."

Mic knew she was beginning to relax in his soft leather seats. He liked her red dress with hints of black sheer in nice places. He could see her skin. Her hair was pushed up in curls that kept trying to escape. He wondered about kissing the red lips.

"Two hundred miles per hour?"

"Yes, it's the only way to travel."

"I'm starving and need some good wine. Maybe a little more speed is what I need. Impact of some sort would change things."

She looked at the man beside her. Tiare wasn't sure the young man realized this date was just dinner. He looked like he was on fire. She knew her responses were dulled by the lack of her friend, Dan, on the premises. She wondered if she could be normal with the new guy. "What was normal?"

Entertaining her with racing stories at the restaurant, Mic smiled. She leaned toward him. It was getting late. She told him a little bit about her relationship with Dan. Her story was surface stuff but enough to change the color of everything. Mic was given the advantage. She shared.

"We met, because of an old boyfriend, whom I loved very much, and who married someone else. I was in the throes of an *I-don't-care attitude* when we were dating. I was at an interesting break in my life. It was exciting being around the track teams and people. Then the old boyfriend named Mark Draydon, and his wife separated. I got back together with him, the old boyfriend."

Mic frowned and shook his head. He was having difficulty seeing how a second go-around could work.

"My friend, Dan, from the race track was super mad at me for a long time. Next the old boyfriend left me and went back to the wife. The problem was this happened twice. We finally became friends despite the disasters. On occasion, I do see the old boyfriend when there is time in Los Angeles. We are still good friends, too."

"Your story sounds like the same soap opera of my past marriages." He recognized the hang-dog attitude on Dan. Dan was part of the leftovers. Heck, it was the same place Mic resided. Mic didn't want to be in that zone again. He had moved on. He bet Dan wanted to move on, too, except here was Tiare.

"Mic, let's not talk about those other people. I'm not in the mood. Why do you like racing so much? Is it because of the racing fans?"

"No, my game is always the track. The curve of the track and noise are entertainment. The stands and fans help add to the picture. But there is the black-checkered flag and money—allure personified. Anyway, I'm very good at judging other driver's moves, and I like the speed. No, let me correct myself. I more than love the speed and anything with heart. You have heart. I could feel yours beat when we first met."

Tiare knew it was time to end their dinner date. The man was on a roll. Lonely men talked about heart. She was tired of talking and didn't have time to mend someone. His file was full of broken lives. She was on a police case and the man was her subject. Things were complicated. She wouldn't allow interference to happen on her first real case.

Mic parked the car at her hotel and walked her back to her room which was next to Tami's room with an open-door passage between them.

"You might think I am fast, but I was never known to be a slow person. My life moves at the same speed that I drive my cars. I made a room reservation in the room directly below your room in case you were interested in spending the night in private. I would love to be with you. I feel very connected to you and when I helped your lightweight body up the step of my motorhome, everything clicked. There was an ignition spark, and my arms wanted to hold you. I would love to explore those feelings in a potentially exciting relationship. I thought we could make a good team. We should take the time to find out. Hoping you feel the same, I made the reservation just in case."

Now Mic knew he was talking too much.

Tiare was warned about Mic, the playboy, by Tami and Rhonda, but she felt the same spark he talked about. She was surprised by this man's effect on her feelings. She hadn't known that feeling for some time. It was too early to let him know how she felt. She made her decision.

"No, I don't want to mix my private life with business. However, I do know the room number."

He couldn't help himself. She was wise enough to know about the special rigged hotel room for a potential woman of his dreams. Suddenly, Mic pulled her into his arms in the hotel hallway and gave her his very best, killer kiss. The kiss almost worked until she told him goodnight and closed the door. He thought about knocking on her door but decided to let her make the next move. He looked at the painted wood door of her room and lightly banged his head on the frame. Knowing a caution flag was waving in his face, Mic hoped he wasn't out of the race. He left, disheartened.

About one in the morning, Mic was still awake thinking about Tiare. He heard a light knock on his glass patio door which connected to the balcony. The room was on the eighth floor. He wondered who was out there. He picked up the lamp for a weapon and pulled the drape.

Surprised to see Tiare untying a black climbing rope from around her waist and wearing black knit pajama pants and top, he saw her hair was banded into a tight top knot out of the way of the rope. She wore a diamond stud in her belly button. He wondered what other pieces were pierced and would find out. Mic put down the lamp and quickly opened the sliding door.

Not wanting Tiare to change her crazy mind, he thought her second entrance into his life was a little more than unreal. Impressions did always matter to him, and she hit them out of the park twice. He punched the remote button to turn the TV soft music station on. Mic enveloped her into his tanned arms, kissing her red lips, and gladly losing the night until dawn in exchange for something sweeter. There was no need for conversation until they satisfied their urgent desire for each other. Passion was overtaking their young, strong and firm bodies. Two hearts were racing.

He would permanently rent the hotel room for his time in Michigan and give her the second key. Mic didn't want Tiare to enter the room the way she came in. The fall from the balcony was a long way down, even though she looked extremely skilled at rappelling and climbing. He wanted her to enter their room the normal route. Abnormal could happen later.

4   Race Track Tires

THE MAN SLIPPED quietly into the track, using his stolen badge key, to access the garage area. Taking his special tool, he targeted two of the drivers, one tire each. He would slip in again if these two attempts didn't create a mess. The cameras did a sweep and caught an image of the man. The extra cameras were part of the new security requested by the police for their investigation into the poisoning crime against the race car driver named Mic Palla.

The next morning Dan saw Tiare and intercepted her.

"I hope you feel better today, and I was sorry to hear from your security person that you canceled dinner with me because of the flu. I would like to know if you want to go out this evening. That is, if you are feeling better?"

Tiare's eyes squinted when she realized what Mic did to get a date with her. "I'm truly up for dinner this evening with you, but you must keep our date a surprise from everyone."

"Sure, I'm game. Meet you at the French restaurant and we'll do the same time."

Tiare went to her meeting with Jim and Tami for their conference call with Derek and Rhonda. They would update Derek on their findings and learn about the Snake woman's island. The Snake woman worked exclusively with the Mamba snake poison.

Of course, Dan bragged a little when he met Mic at the concession stand about his next date with the pretty red-headed woman named Tiare. Mic congratulated Dan on his finesse in getting a date.

"I heard that this woman was very difficult to nail down for a date and even more so about allowing a man into her bed."

Dan looked at Mic and laughed. "Women never were a problem for me. You haven't met this super girl. But then I own all the right equipment like brains, brawn, and insight to match a woman's every desire, especially someone like Tiare. We are exceptionally good friends if you know what I mean."

"Is that so?"

"Yes, everyone knows about our relationship and besides they make things bigger in Texas. That's the draw for super girl."

Mic was thinking about Tiare and Dan's comments. Bigger head was what he was thinking and no brains. However, Mic was upset she was a super girl with competitor jock boy. The more he thought about the two of them together, the more distracted he became at the track.

He needed to correct the situation shortly or he would mess up his driving times with his failure to concentrate. Mic didn't want Tiare around Dan. He didn't like being around Dan on the race track and maneuvered his car around him whenever possible. On the track, he figured out how to win car slot numbers in front of him by driving higher timed speeds. He would now have to figure a way to out-maneuver him away from super girl.

Neither driver required new tires that day, so the tire puncture person would need to wait another day to view his results. The wrong video security tape was sent to the police to monitor. The police would eventually catch the fact that they received the same tape twice which was identical to the day before.

Tiare and Dan went to their dinner. Mic followed them to the new French restaurant. Mic was familiar with the restaurant having been there before. He slipped into the bar and ordered a drink. Waiting until they ate their main meal, he watched as the hooker Mic hired sat down at Dan's table. The hooker knew Dan intimately from a previous dinner at the same restaurant.

When he saw Tiare stand up, glare at Dan, walk to the lobby, and reach for her cell phone to call for a taxi, Mic sauntered out of the bar.

"Hello, fancy meeting you here. Wasn't it like getting a royal flush in a five-card poker game with no replacement card? The odds were six hundred forty-nine thousand seven hundred forty to one. Those are absolutely and positively amazing odds. Do you require a lift? I'm going back to the hotel."

Tiare looked at Mic and knew he was somehow responsible for her disastrous evening. He looked guilty. She felt like the little red-cloaked girl in the storybook. The wolf was standing in front of her.

"The word strange comes to mind about our second encounter in a row. Wouldn't that somehow change your odds story to a higher number? Unless the wolf ate your calculator, too."

Mic just whistled. It dawned on him that he was the wolf in her story. He tried to smile.

Tiare relented and accepted his ride but didn't come to his room that evening. Mic knew he messed up and would need to figure a way back into her good graces. Perhaps he did her a favor by pointing out the other man's weaknesses. He told himself that he didn't think she appreciated those facts at all. Mic would need to talk with Tami, her sister, to gain her help and confidence. Tami could be a knowledgeable asset.

After that evening, Tiare saw Mic as a bad boy. Mic would not be in a good mood due to his break with her. It was something he hadn't counted on. Now he was more distracted at the track.

Nor would Dan be in a good mood when he found out who hired the hooker. When Dan's tire blew the next day, damaging his car, he thought Mic fixed his tire somehow. Mic, however, didn't fix anybody's cars or tires, because those activities would lose his reputation at the tracks and take away his most favorite thing in the world to do which was racing the top circuits.

Mic hadn't yet used his ill-fated tire.

5   Dan's Tire Wreck

DAN STEPPED INTO his race car and drove the machine to his designated position for another timed lap on the track. He finished the lap and was slowing down on the incline when his front tire blew, throwing him into a spinout on the tracks with his car eventually stopped near the center grass. The race car sunk into the wet earth; the wheels were down to the axle in the soft black dirt. The front of his car nicked one of the parked media vans that were hired for an advertising video of him. Tow trucks were required to pull both vehicles out.

"What the heck happened with the tire? There was an odd jolt before my tire blew, and we hit each other."

His pit crew and officials ran over to survey the damage. There was a burn on the tire in a long streak which wasn't normal. The officials contacted security and the police. There would need to be an investigation. The rest of the runs were canceled for the day.

Tiare went to the track and had talked with Dan earlier. She watched his run and was shooting her own video on her cell phone. She rechecked the video. She sent the video to Tami and Jim who immediately came to the inner track to help investigate the scene. Tiare turned to move in their direction when Mic saw her.

Tiare refrained from talking to him for a day and a half. The time was too long for Mic. His patience wore thin and his fragmented world needed to stop spinning. He leaped over the bleachers to reach her. He grabbed her arm.

"We need to talk."

"Not now."

Mic blocked her path down the step.

"Yes, right now. Let the other investigators handle the tire and accident business."

Tiare sent Tami a short text. They went back to Mic's motorhome. He kicked his security people outside because of a private conversation that was required.

"Do you want a drink?"

"No, yes, no. It's too early. I will take a couple of olives. I need ones with the pits in them just in case my weapon doesn't work."

"Testy today?"

He took a gamble and made her a martini anyway. She slowly sipped the drink because she knew the tire in the video showed a small explosion. The blown tire was no accident. Tiare was worried about Dan and the other drivers. Mic saw her concern and thought her feelings were only about Dan.

"I'm tired of the cold shoulder. I did apologize to you and sincerely meant it. I miss our conversations plus lots of other things too numerous to mention. I'm sure you know what those other things are that I am talking about. My past relationships have been reckless, but you are not in my past. You are currently someone worth my every moment of time. You are all I think about."

"I do remember." She stopped talking.

"See, there you go again, talking to me in clipped conversation. I receive those same verbal cues from my ex-wives. I hate that war stuff with women. A man never wins, and there begins a cycle of blame and guilt. I don't want communication failure in our relationship because I'm starting to fall in love with you. I am done with throw-away relationships. I want someone who knows I am worth it. You were letting me know that information hot and heavy that first night. I want you to believe in me. Did I say I love you very much because it is the truth? I meant all those words I told you last night, too. I have no clue how the whole thing between us happened, but flames start every time I'm near you. I believe you feel the same flare."

Tiare looked at him and the drink was having an effect. Her eyes started tearing up.

"Oh, man, now I made you cry. My words shouldn't cause this reaction. Now I'm confused."

Mic went over to her, held her close while putting his face into her hair, and he looked deeply into her eyes.

"I was worried and nervous," said Tiare.

"You were worried about Dan?"

"I'm worried about you."

Mic shook his head. "We blow tires all day long. The numerous trips around the curves wear them out plus the junk on the track. Or am I missing something?"

"The tire may have been rigged with some type of injectable explosive which would explode when the device reached a certain temperature. You need to have your tires checked immediately and any in your racks. I was worried that this explosive might have been a let-me-get-your-attention job. We seem to have a new player in the game. This con artist or jerk wants to scare you a little bit to put you on edge. I believe the target was really aimed at you, again."

"Seriously, I don't believe the tire rigging idea and now two players want to do me in?"

She pulled out her phone and showed him the video.

Mic enlarged the car and replayed the images over and over.

"Oh, nuts, that's what I need. This person is some crazed, rotten fan on the loose. In a race, blown tires would be a bigger mess on the tracks. This person must know that Dan and I are very competitive but then most of the fans already know those facts. We don't exactly hide our animosity."

"Yes, the next situation could be bad. The police and investigators need to catch the person fast before they get a second wind. If we don't, he or she could also get in the way. I disagree on the loose fan. This new jerk was probably not a fan. Fans don't get this sophisticated. We are dealing with someone who has knowledge of the race tracks, explosives, and how to gain access. Our main objective here is catching the poisoner, and she doesn't normally use explosives. This new incident is somebody else."

Tiare thought this episode was only the beginning of more incidents at the race tracks. Plus, the fan crowd would increase after each race. The fans might hope to catch a little bit of action on their home videos and would want to see the show. The higher the crowd, the more difficult for security and the police to catch someone who was illusive like a snake.

"Two snakes, a big one and a small one," said Tiare.

Mic looked at Tiare. They were both quiet. She hadn't mentioned Dan. He was glad. He bent down and kissed her knowing she forgave him some of his little misdeeds. There were other larger things to worry about.

"Do you still have the hotel key?"

Tiare smiled and looked at Mic. "You'll have to wait and see. Perhaps you should kiss me a little more just to make sure I won't forget. The words of love did help."

Mic smiled, "Of course, anything my lovely woman wants. I'm immediately yours. I recommend room service for dinner tonight."

"I agree to room service, but now I must get back to the tire investigation."

"Yes, I'll walk you back to the stands. I'm glad we talked. Whew, now I can get my concentration back into the game."

The young people strolled through the gated area and went back to the track. Mic occasionally touched her hands or back to escort her. There were always media people around the track. He wanted to be careful about showing affection in the open. This was the way he treated most women. Anything more and the media would immediately know she was worth interviewing and descend upon her. He didn't want to share her just yet, and he thought about her comment on snakes. He was starting to feel strange and looked behind him. Mic would need to be careful now Tiare was in his life. He was wrapped in serious bad crap. Snakes were sinister.

6   Plan to Catch a Criminal

JIM MICHAELS CONTACTED Derek Wright. The problems were getting bigger than anyone figured. Two suspects unrelated to each other could be distracting.

"There was a problem at the track today with one of the driver's tires. The car was one of Dan Jaehn's vehicles. Dan was driving when the tire burst, and a media truck was taking a video, but they were shooting the left side of the vehicle. Their camera didn't catch the pop. My guess is an injectable or putty explosive was placed in or on a front right tire. Tiare's video shows clearly the blast."

"I believe you are correct. The video was more than interesting. Did the police review the security tapes?"

"There was a problem sending the correct tape, but this has been resolved. The police were reviewing the tapes from the past three days. The badge swipes to the pit area were also recorded. If there is anything strange with the workers, the device should register the badge number of the individual."

Jim said, "The rest of the right front tire was removed, and the track was swept and bagged. The federal agency picked the tire and track mess up. After checking the other three tires on a hoist, there was nothing wrong with them. The blast area was small and tight on the race car."

Derek sighed. "Let me know their findings and I know the police and other agency will want to set a trap for the rest of the week to see if the person repeats his puncture of tires. I'll contact and ask my superiors to talk with the Michigan federal people. The criminal might be the type to follow a pattern. There could be other tires punctured, but I thought the right front tire made sense to blow on the track. The turn of the wheel by the driver would immediately throw the car in a spin from a blown right tire placing the vehicle in front of all drivers riding the pole. Since the right tires are clearly marked in the bins, the pit crews could allow you inside to check each next day's tires for the drivers before their lap run. You could dress as an official. Your appearance will not be questioned about being in the pit area."

Derek was glad the news van hadn't caught the tire video like Tiare did. "Don't disclose any information about our findings to the media. Facts about an explosive can be released later. Let others believe the delay in test runs was only a normal blown-tire incident."

"This person's motives could be anything. He could be targeting a specific set of top drivers or at least the newsworthy ones. There could be a psycho on the loose trying to get famous. Or there could be someone trying to throw the race, and they were testing the explosive first. The answers aren't there for us to determine the objective at this point."

Derek knew Jim was more than likely correct in his assessment.

31

"Get with the police to ask them to delay information to the media. The longer the time, the better, and I'll work my end."

"I'm on it with the police and security at the track. I hope our suspect is a normal psycho this time."

"Thanks, but I don't think so. This is someone intelligent in the game, unrelated to why we are here. The game is usually about money or rather, a lack of the green stuff."

"One other little problem exists. Tiare is dating Mic. Mic reserved a room at their hotel directly below Tiare's room. Per Tami, our girl usually disappeared later in the evening. Dan also has the hots for the girl."

"Now, we will need to guard all three of them from people outside and inside the tracks. Do you need extra people?"

"It might not be a bad idea to send two more people into the investigation with the current situation."

Derek said, "I will let you know who and when they will arrive. My new hire might be free from wrapping up a current case and possibly Rhonda."

"That's great because I do like both Rhonda Peters and Brandon Keller."

"Rhonda will be relieved that Mic has a new focus."

"Right on."

Derek shook his head after getting off the phone.

7   Possible Known Criminal

THE SECOND DAMAGED tire was found in Mic's rack of tires and the police were notified. A special crew came to the track to remove the tire and run tests to verify the type of device used. Tami and Jim talked with Mic at his motorhome. Tiare needed to return to Los Angeles for the weekend and was not involved in the meeting.

"Did you know of anyone who might want to harm you using the race track and explosives as their venue?"

"No, I don't recall anyone. I do remember a race car driver from five years ago, that used to work in the armed forces before joining the circuit."

"We need the person's name, so we can discuss some things with the police and ask his whereabouts recently."

"I thought I saw this person at the track the other day, but time changes a person's looks. I wasn't sure if he was the same person."

Tami looked at Jim. "We need the name. This person might be important. Also, did the other driver, Dan, know this same person?"

"Yes, we both raced against the man. The driver was as good as we were back then. The three of us were cocky and dangerous. We were younger and took more

33

risks in our driving. Dan and I were better and maneuvered around him which pissed the guy off. We pissed him off whenever our times were better. Most of the time, he placed in front of us."

"The other guy's team and manager ran into problems with the race officials and the organization. They were always losing points and getting fined for violations. There were roof flap problems or improper attachment mounts and supports. Sometimes they were kicked out of the race for the day."

Tami raised her eyebrows at Jim.

Jim said, "Go on."

"I remember their last race. Two of their cars were out due to violations during inspection. There was only the one car left. Both Dan and I bumped the guy's car in passing which made him mad. The guy stepped on the gas in the straightaway. I saw him coming and did a block move, but I wasn't very successful. He hit the wall and totaled the car. I spun out of the race with little damage. The other guy's sponsors didn't renew the contract with his manager or any member of their team. No other sponsors would touch them due to their shenanigans. In this business, if there's no backing money, a person is out of the big powerhouse league of racing. The last time I heard, the other guy was doing a little stock car racing and some pit work on the junk tracks. I'm not sure where the manager went or if he's working. The rest of the crew eventually did join other teams on the circuit and are racing in the big leagues today."

Tami responded, "We need all the names now."

"Sure, I can provide them. The driver is Trent Rudy."

Jim wrote down the names and they thanked Mic. Mic stopped Tami.

"Do you know where Tiare is staying in Los Angeles?"

Tami knew Tiare's plans, but she never asked her to be quiet about them. She liked Mic and figured it would be all right because they were, after all, dating. She would use that in her defense if Tiare got mad at her.

"Yes, the place is the Rigger Hotel which happens to be a few blocks from Manhattan Beach in California. It's one of her favorite places due to the closeness to the beach. A person can run the length of the beach in the morning. She likes to catch some rays on a weekend. There are lots of local bands playing at the bars and great seafood restaurants in the area."

"Is the old boyfriend in town?"

"Yes, I heard Mark Draydon was visiting Los Angeles. His mother lives there and he handles her investments. I personally don't like the man."

"Although I haven't met him, I don't like the man either," responded Mic.

Tami and Jim left to investigate the list of names and involve Derek.

Mic drove his sports car to the airport with one of his security people. They were flying to Los Angeles. Their reservations were at the Rigger Hotel. Mic called one of his band buddies to ask which hotel he was playing and reserved two tables. Next, he made

Saturday night dinner reservations at the friend's hotel for two tables. He contacted a local jeweler to purchase a diamond bracelet for Tiare and asked that they deliver the box to the Rigger Hotel to await his arrival. He knew he was going to need the present.

Mic was going to fix the boyfriend appearance problem real soon. If he had to invite the guy to dinner and music, he wanted to be prepared so he would stay in her good graces. He knew how to fake friendship with men. Men did that move all the time.

He was upset with Tiare that she didn't entrust him with her schedule. He thought he knew why. The woman was still carrying a torch for the problem boyfriend. Mic would have stopped her, and she knew it. He thought the man wasn't good enough for her as did a lot of other people. He made his tentative plan for the weekend which included time with Tiare. Mic would show her how much he loved her. He already talked with his attorney about possibilities.

8 Tracker Poisoner, New Murder

DEREK WAS REVIEWING the notes regarding his private conversation with Rhonda Peters about the Miami tracker murder. It was hard for him to call Rhonda by her married name. Sometimes he referred to her as Rhonda White which was her single name. Rhonda occasionally helped Derek with investigations because he paid her well and she really enjoyed the job. Technically, she was a freelance person available to work with the police, but she mostly worked for him. She and her husband, Skid Peters, were good friends with the Wrights.

Interview notes and conversation read as follows:

Explaining to Rhonda the information he received from the Miami police and the strange death, he showed her a copy of the deposit pages. She saw her name and the amount of twenty-five thousand dollars. The money was the amount she paid for an investigator to track her superman boyfriend.

"This period was when I was in my crazy phase worrying about the activities of my boyfriend. I knew something was very wrong. My boyfriend would be gone frequently on trips, but I was gone frequently as well. There was a feeling about him which was off. I saw an ad in a Miami newspaper for investigative services. Having met with a man, I signed a contract for their services, and gave them my check. The person seemed like a man, but I wasn't sure. They followed my boyfriend, took photographs of him with four other women, and gave me an extensive report, including a background check."

"Do you have the document and canceled check?"

"Yes, my accountant keeps my files."

I handed her a release form which she signed to allow me access to the information. The information would be handed over to the Miami detective.

"Can you meet with a police sketch artist soon. We can get a bulletin out about the possible photo of the roommate?"

"Yes, I will do so."

He showed her the photo of the dead woman with the even stranger tattoo. Rhonda shook her head, because she never saw anything like it.

"The rope and snake tattoo are a custom job, successfully executed. Whoever did the ink most definitely would not share the client's real name, because there may be more than one person in the group who wore the design."

"That is an interesting speculation. I will let the detective in Miami know. The detectives liked seeing your happy face in the wedding photographs."

Rhonda remembered one of the wedding photographs. "Yes, they used to like to watch my legs."

"I think you need to inform Skid of our meeting, but probably not the detective's heated comments."

"Yes, my husband knows some of the stories about the unfaithful boyfriend, but not the part about a hired investigator. He also knows about the Miami detectives."

"I'm sorry you must involve Skid; but from a man's perspective, a husband would understand, especially if he can handle the Miami boys."

I wrote down the name of the old boyfriend, totally surprised when Rhonda told me. The name was a familiar one in Miami. The person was part of the very rich elite families. The ability to get any information from the man would be limited by the family's string of company lawyers. It would be a delicate line for the Miami police to walk.

This is the end of the interview.

Derek was glad he would be out of the game in solving the bizarre case in Miami until Mic Palla's strange poisoning in Los Angeles happened.

"I believe there is a heavy connection to the woman who photographed you and Skid. She was murdered in Miami and Mic's incident with the poison has us worried. We must find a connection."

What he didn't know was that a new crime was just committed in Los Angeles while he was reviewing the file. A woman who was married to a politician was shot after she bought her tall cinnamon latte with whipped cream from a nearby coffee house. She was talking with her husband on her cell phone when she saw a woman with a rope tattoo on her neck. Then she saw the gun. The husband heard one shot and pedestrians screaming on his cell. He called the emergency 911 number, but the shot was in the heart. The woman didn't make it.

The police would be involved in solving two murders and yet another piece of an old stolen car case. The slain politician's wife owned a yellow sports car which was stolen earlier in the year from the Grand Oak Clubhouse and Restaurant. She let her boyfriend drive her car for the afternoon. It was the same vehicle Allen and Alex Jackson from the San Francisco crony families chased while in an undercover operation for the police and Derek Wright. They lost track of the yellow car and the thieves.

Some of the parts of the yellow sports car were found later. The parts were on the chop-shop floor which was captured by the police in a case involving a man named Minnow Surf and his band of women. The women stole sports cars for Minnow. A Los Angeles man bought the yellow car's parts and another red sports car with a damaged door at a police auction. The parts and door were used to rebuild the other sports car he purchased which were the same make and model. The LA man was none other than Trent Rudy. His name was on the Miami woman's accounting books as a client for services and the name was circled. The registered, separate VIN number found did match the dead Miami tracker woman's red sports car. Rudy sold the rebuilt car to her.

The dead politician's wife was listed as the original owner of the yellow sports car. Her husband bought her the car while on a trip to Germany. The yellow sports car was shipped to the U.S. as a surprise. Now that she was permanently in the morgue from an unsolved murder, the report Derek received much later was extensive, including information about the husband politician.

The husband politician was originally from a well-known family in Miami. Derek recognized the name again. It was the former superman boyfriend that Rhonda had dated. The politician moved to Los Angeles to enter the political arena. Leaving Miami meant the politician dropped a few of his girlfriends. His new image was important to match his clean political aspirations. Rhonda would be valuable in providing information because she knew the man intimately.

Derek would become re-engaged in the aspects of the possible connection to the dead Miami woman, the dead LA politician's wife, the wife's boyfriend, the very much alive politician husband, the buyer which was Trent Rudy, and now the race car driver named Mic. From the police viewpoint, it looked like a simple lover-murder case on the Los Angeles side. They were looking at the woman's boyfriend. The other murder was probably a competitor fight over some sort of investigative services involving a woman with snake tattoos in Miami. *But what about Mic?*

Derek knew better. There was nothing simple to murder. He would need to untangle the mess and all the connections. Knowledge of the other real Snake woman would resurface. Derek wouldn't be able to connect her to the politician or the dead wife. Either she was very good or wasn't involved. Husbands were always suspects that led nowhere. He needed solid proof and the clues were a minefield of quicksand. Someone had to know something. The Trent Rudy guy was in the game and Derek knew it. Now was the time to find the man and interview him.

The case would become total chaos. It was one of the worse he encountered. Derek was getting a headache and gave up. He needed his wife's insight. Jess knew the criminal mind and should have been a police profiler. She thought like a criminal when she was involved in several of his past cases. She loved to catch the psycho person, out-thinking them was her specialty. He also wondered if Ara's psychologist friend, Rosemary Quinn, would be any help. According to Ara, the woman was creative at figuring out a person's psyche.

9   Former Race Car Driver Talk

BRANDON AND DEREK flew to Michigan and found the former race car driver sitting in the stands. Jim pointed him out to them. Derek recognized an older version of the man from the photo they received. A room was reserved for the meeting and a local police investigator walked with them. The man tried to flee when he saw three people descending upon his area of seats.

"Why do they always run?"

Brandon looked at Derek who answered his cell. The two police handcuffed and escorted the man to the meeting room.

"We are good to go."

Derek sat down in the chair across from the man and crossed his legs in a relaxed posture.

"You do know people run when they are guilty. It's a reflex reaction to the law and all its rules. By the way, I'm Derek Wright, a Los Angeles investigator. My partner here is Brandon Keller. We have some questions for a person whose name is Trent Rudy. Our understanding is that you are this person, and we have some questions about parts and a red sports car you purchased at a police auction while living in California."

"I'm Trent and the sports car parts were a legal transaction which I fully paid in cash to the police. The California police wouldn't take checks or credit cards

43

at the auction. It's a miracle that they sell anything at them places. I go to other auctions like in Arizona, and they don't make me anti-up money to purchase car engines. We know those people in the desert carry bigger guns than the police. The whole state is full of the crazies. So only a fool would stiff them in an auction with a bad check or a stolen credit card. Therefore, why are you questioning me here? I'm all legal and I was minding my own business sitting in the stands. This is Michigan. Can't a guy get a break in this state? You need to harass me here, too. When I saw you three unfriendly people approaching and two of you were wearing ties, I did run. Nobody normal wears a tie anymore other than lawyers going to court. And nobody at the tracks in Michigan wear them either, despite the cold. If they do wear one, it's one of those hand-knit wool jobs, usually green and white. Do you watch football? Your ties, they are slick and red-colored silk. Silk means serious stuff. Do I need a lawyer?"

"I'll have to tell my friends at the police station about your complaint with their auction practices. They will love writing your name down. Perhaps they can talk to you next time you arrive at their auction."

Derek flipped his tie over.

"It does say silk and yes, we do watch football."

Derek and Brandon saw the man squirm a little. He knew the investigators were playing him.

"Of course, we are in Michigan and who doesn't like the game," said Brandon.

Derek turned to Brandon. "It isn't cold enough for green and white wool ties. Besides, we should have asked for some lawyer cards while we were at the local police station here."

Brandon nodded, and Derek turned back to the man sitting at the track room table.

"You can pay expensive fees to lawyers or not. The decision is yours," said Derek.

"Okay, can we cut the three-way small talk? I was just trying to be friendly with conversation. What type of questions? I don't want to spend my money on some cheap lawyer."

"You gave a woman in Miami a huge asset because the transfer shows one dollar, and then she paid you money back to the tune of fifty thousand dollars. Your name was on her list of clients and of course, there was the transfer of the red sports car to her by you. Her name was Coral Hanson. Can you provide us more information about your transaction with her?"

Trent picked up on the one word. "You said was?"

"The woman is dead," commented Brandon.

Trent sat back in his chair. "Well, I didn't kill her. The car was a partial gift. It was included in some investigative services she did for me. But then she paid me for the extra work that I did on the rebuild. She wanted expensive everything on that car. I know nothing else about the woman."

"You gave an eighty-five-thousand-dollar vehicle to a woman you barely knew? That's what we believe is a little suspicious and the laundering of more money across the table." Derek left the room to let Trent Rudy sweat a little bit.

XXXXXX

Trent knew that he needed to throw a little smoke at their butts. He was good at lying. Where in the world did that Derek person go? When Derek entered the room. Trent decided his next move.

"I asked for information about a guy named Minnow Surf who sold parts to people. I wanted to bypass the police auction price and save some money in rebuilding future cars. The woman wanted me to get a second car for her. We did a business deal except I lied and told her the first car was not traceable or involved in any crime. That was why the Miami woman wanted to do the deal and keep the business investment. If she's dead, then I don't need to get her a second car."

Derek and Brandon both said, "Unbelievable."

Derek also saw the man squint his eyes. They weren't sure where he picked up Minnow's name, but thought it was probably from the newspaper coverage regarding Mr. Surf's death. Or maybe the Miami dead woman provided the name to Trent. Derek mentioned the date and time of death for the Miami woman.

Trent's eyes were dilated. "I wasn't there in Miami until the next day."

The two men knew the person in front of them was a lying piece of crap.

"How did she die?"

Derek handed him a picture of the dead woman that showed her tattoo. "Suffocation was the cause. Have you ever seen this tattoo before?"

Trent knew the tattoo marking but wasn't going to say anything. He thought the other roommate wore one. "No," he replied curtly.

"You also purchased the car parts to a yellow sports car which originally belonged to a politician's wife. Her car was stolen."

I did, and the transaction is considered legal."

"We know the transaction was legal, but the politician's wife also died which places you smack dab in the middle of a case of two murdered women," said Derek.

"What's your problem? Is it a crime to want to leave the junk race track and get money rebuilding cars? You know that I used to race, right? Isn't that how you found me? Your spies saw me at the tracks. My job is fixing cars. It's what I'm knowledgeable and super good at doing for a living. It took me a while to figure things out. Is that a crime? Or are you trying to scare me? I've not killed either one of those women and you know it. Everyone knew the politician's wife. I didn't know the parts were from her vehicle. That's why you are trying to point fingers at me. You people don't know either and have no clue whose responsible. Now isn't that funny? I don't have any information for the police. However, perhaps I can sell the lack of police knowledge to the news media. They might find things interesting. I could use the money they will pay me. Understand this, you don't scare me."

Derek did the nod to his partner. Brandon got up and went out of the room for a smoke. The former driver in the interview pissed them both off. The guy was hiding something major. Both investigative partners knew the man was full of defensive moves. Defense was a temporary shield, thin as cheap glass, and easily broken. Brandon knew that it was time to give the floor to Derek.

Derek had hit the record on his cell phone earlier to make sure they captured the conversation for themselves. He would provide the recording to his team later.

"We don't want you to travel very far because you may think of something pertinent to our investigation. We are not the scary people you should worry about."

The former race car driver sneered at Derek now that they were alone. "Got you today, didn't I?"

Derek was knowledgeable in the ways of the bad guys. This person was one of them. The man had no clue the danger he was in.

"You're a tiny rodent compared to the bigger ring of snakes. They are the type to slowly strangle, use large metal bullets, or dump poison in your brain at a slow rate of speed. Whichever method they choose will be full of blinding pain, guaranteed. Go ahead and broadcast your story to the media. Your story will inform the rope snake thugs and any other snake leaders precisely your location."

Derek stood up.

"Oh, I forgot to tell you that there is a larger, more powerful, supremely intelligent poisonous snake person chasing these lesser thugs. She is pissed they copied her routine and probably stole lots of her money. It's not about the money. For her, the next step will probably be about revenge. Perhaps you saw something that puts you into her direct line of sight. The massively superior snake, a true master in her profession, is feared by everyone, including the police. The police may bow out until it's all over, sometimes letting evil do the job for us, especially when we have no information. How do we know these facts? The red sports car and the yellow car were originally stolen. The red car especially led the larger snake directly to your door and the two women. Why don't you go figure out your chances at survival? I'm betting 10-20 percent. That number could be a little on the high side."

Trent stopped listening. He was glad Derek didn't ask about the tires. He speculated about the pop in Dan's tire that he saw. He knew someone who might have hired that job out. He gave the man a loan. The loan money came from the payment he received for an untraceable, rebuilt sports car and a potential second car. Or he thought the cars were untraceable. Rebuilding cars was the only way he could make good money. He owed this other man a favor for throwing a race a long time ago. The man recently came to collect from him.

Trent knew he was a bad boy and so was the other man, but he wondered about the rope snake thugs. He also didn't know there was a master snake.

"I hope I made your situation clear and ours. Goodbye for now Mr. Rudy."

Trent mulled over Derek's words and he started looking over his shoulder. He couldn't help it. He wondered if he might know something. Trent did visit Coral Hanson at her place in Miami and saw her roommate. He wondered if the roommate still lived there. Or was there something about the cars?

"If not, where did you go Miss Roommate. What and who helped you? Who is the master snake? Do you know her, and did she see me? No, they're wrong. I'm safe."

Trent worried that he might be in trouble. The words: *not safe bounced in his brain like a ping pong ball*. He hit the side of his head and could hear the ball flatten. Then the ball rolled back and forth, the crushed edges scraping his left side. He developed a big migraine.

When he got back to his room, Trent took some aspirin, and he made new plans. First, he needed to contact his former manager, the one who was in charge when he raced on the super tracks. His manager's name was Kevin Sawyer. Kevin didn't pay him anything back on the loan of money. Trent hadn't heard from Kevin in months. He was at the Michigan track in the hopes that he would run into Sawyer while there. Trent Rudy didn't see the man at all recently. Retrieval of his money was going to be a more difficult and bigger problem than he thought. He could have given the two investigators Sawyer's name. If he did, there wouldn't ever be repayment. That's why Rudy kept silent. The money was something he couldn't afford to lose permanently.

10   Los Angeles and Tiare

MIC AND HIS security guard checked into their room at the Rigger Hotel. They walked by Tiare's room at eleven o'clock in the evening and her light was still on. There was no rental car in the parking spot in front of her room. Tami told him Tiare sometimes took the bus from the airport and walked where she wanted to go or rented a bicycle at a small shop around the corner from the hotel.

Mic dumped his small suitcase and briefcase in his room and went back to Tiare's room. Her light was turned off. He decided to wait until morning to see her. The meeting between them must appear as a natural occurrence. He could wait, knowing she was tucked in for the evening.

The next morning, he saw her leave her room to go jogging on the beach. Mic sauntered down to the hotel lobby and talked with the desk clerk.

"Where did the local tourists like to go for lunch and a beer that was within walking or biking distance?"

"Oh, the tourists loved to go to Henri's off Bayview Drive and Tenth Street. The food was always the best and there is adequate indoor and outdoor seating, plus they provide locked bicycle racks. A person paid a fee for the lock, and then the restaurant deducts the bicycle lock fee from the lunch ticket. The cyclist crowd loves to eat there."

"Did the pretty woman in room number six ask about this restaurant?"

"No, she has stayed here at the hotel many times before and visited the restaurant called Henri's. But yesterday she asked me where Bruno's was located. It's a newer restaurant. She explained that she was meeting a close friend. Of course, I helped her with the address location. You see the airlines held up her luggage which was where she stored her cell phone cord, and she couldn't recharge. The use of the cell phone's navigation was dead on her device. Mine worked just fine to locate the restaurant. But the airline should deliver her luggage today. Then she will be all set."

Mic was glad the airline messed with her luggage. The loss was a perfect set up to ask the next round of questions. "Where exactly is this Bruno's place and is the dress code casual?"

"Yes, the place is an Italian-Renaissance, very delightful, casually upscale restaurant off Ocean Drive and Twelfth Street. They do have sidewalk seating available. All that is required are average tourist clothes, shorts, and flip-flops. You do need something with soles. They serve cold beer, wine, the best Bloody Mary around, and vegetable juice. Then their pasta is super excellent, also. Meat or no meat, the sauce is gourmet quality. Dessert is currently mixed fresh fruit on top of homemade dough. Their whipped cream is to-die-for."

The hotel clerk rolled his eyes. "Massive real organic vanilla." The man sighed.

"Organic, wow! The restaurant food sounds delightful. My friends and I might like to eat there. Did she say what time she was going to lunch? I imagine the time the restaurant first opens would be best. A person would beat the crowds. I bet there are crowds with the interesting menu items you mentioned?"

"Yes, the restaurant fills quickly. You will want to get there early. The place opens at eleven. I could ask her what time?"

Mic was pleased. "No, thank you. Her boyfriend must be important. I can meet my date and friend there early so eleven works just fine for us. I really appreciate your help. If you ever need tickets to a race, like possibly Fontana, let me know. I'm a race fan big time."

"I do like racing. Here's my card. You can mail me tickets any time. Have a very good day, sir."

Tiare rode her bicycle to the restaurant and selected a corner outside table. Mark Draydon arrived, and she stood up. He quickly kissed her.

"Sit down, Tiare, because I have exciting news."

The waiter arrived quickly. His news would have to wait. They decided to order drinks, and both ordered their favorite pasta and salad. The drinks were brought immediately. Tiare ordered white wine with Alfredo noodles and sauce. They decided to share a Caesar Salad. Mark wanted to try the shortcake.

Mark ordered marinara pasta and a Bloody Mary. His mother bought him a new slack and shirt outfit for his birthday which he wore this morning for their date. He informed Tiare about a meeting with clients after lunch.

"Hello, how are you?"

"I'm absolutely great and business is doing even better. Oh, remind me to order the dessert later."

"Yes, I will. I'm glad to hear that information about your business. Is your mother feeling better?"

"My mother is better and talks about you. There are her favorite things and she wants to go shopping tomorrow."

Tiare didn't want to go shopping with his mother. She hoped that he wasn't setting her up to handle the task like he had done in the past. Tiare wanted sunshine and freedom before going back to Michigan. If she went shopping, it would be alone. She started racking up excuses in her brain. The two finished their salad and the pasta was delivered. Tiare felt better until she saw who walked into the restaurant.

Mic, his security guard, and a tall blonde woman sat down at a table for four people. Their table was one table down from theirs on the inside, close to the building. A waiter quickly came to take their orders.

Tiare was stunned to see Mic at the other table with a woman. She stopped listening to Mark. She wondered what Mic could possibly be doing in Los Angeles with a blonde. Why didn't he tell her about the meeting? Perhaps he had talked with Jim or Tami. But then, she never told Mic about her plans either. What

55

was the word, touché or back-at-you? She didn't know how to react.

Mark started his story.

"We are separating again which means that I am free to date and the first person that came to my mind was you. I thought we can begin our wonderful relationship again like before. I can meet you in Michigan or wherever and sometimes you can come to Los Angeles to stay at my mother's home. There is plenty of room, so you won't need a car or hotel room. What do you think? We can start immediately and have dinner together like old times. I miss our evenings together very much."

Mic looked up and saw Tiare watching him. He jumped up from his chair and came over to her table.

"If the stars just didn't align today and brought the two of us together in the same city. What are the odds of that happening? It is about the same odds as finding the lost city called Atlantis. Hi, my love, it is good to see you."

Mic turned to Mark and introduced himself.

Mark looked balefully at Mic. "I'm impressed that Tiare knows a race car driver again. She seems to collect them on occasion, but then she throws them away. Don't you darling?"

Mark threw a look at the man who interfered with his nice conversation.

Mic wasn't fazed by the man's got-you-in-the-face-Casanova look.

Tiare stopped eating and stared at the two men. She was their tug-of-war. There were two Casanovas staring at her and both were blatantly sparring.

"The woman obviously has good taste. That's why I see her at the race tracks. It is nice talking with you, Tiare, but I need to return to my friend. She is helping me with party arrangements. We'll see you later."

Mic looked directly at Tiare. He went back to his table to discuss this evening's setup. The woman was an old band friend's wife.

Mark took hold of Tiare's hand, "Did you hear what I did mention earlier?"

Tiare was brought back to reality. "You said we. The topic was your old wife. You and I are the we in your sentence. I vaguely caught that you are separated again. This is new information. I thought that I was only meeting a friend. Now you want more than a friend. Is this the third time? Why is it the third time anyway?"

Tiare was upset by Mic and upset by the situation she was forced into by Mark. She felt pushed and pulled by both men.

Mark knew she was still mad about the last time he returned to his wife. He kissed Tiare's hand and held her fingers with both of his hands.

"You know that there was an important reason why I helped her for a while after the divorces. She needed me. My tenderness was important, but now my wife has found someone else. Isn't that delightful that she is moving onward? Her action opened the door. I'm a believer again. Everything can be fine between us. That's why I am here."

Mark kissed Tiare's hand again, slowly kissing her bare ring finger.

Mic didn't like the way the guy was hanging onto Tiare or touching her. The man was driving him bonkers. He saw the waiter approaching with their order of red wine, Bloody Mary, and cold iced-glass of beer with a side shot of tequila. The cost on the tray was only twenty-five dollars. Mic made his decision. He pointed, nodded, and motioned to the guy named Mark. His security guard knew what those gestures meant. They did this trick once before.

His security guard quickly stood up in front of the waiter who tipped the tray the wrong direction. The security guard tried to grab the tray, accidentally tilting it toward Mark. Fortunately, the drinks were in heavy-duty, restaurant grade plastic glasses and mugs. There was no breakage. The glasses went flying and the liquids hit Mark squarely in the upper torso. The beige shirt and slacks were soaked in beer, tequila, vodka, and red stuff. All the patrons in the outdoor seating section paused. A car honked a horn and everyone at the restaurant restarted their conversations.

Mark dropped Tiare's hand and felt the cold liquid permeate through his clothes. He gasped and grabbed his wallet, throwing down fifty dollars.

"Sorry, but I must race home and change before I meet my clients. We can talk again. I'll contact you later."

Both Mic's security man and the waiter were apologizing profusely and handing over napkins to help the guy who pushed them out of his way while leaving.

Mic invited Tiare to join their table and finish her meal.

"No, I want to catch some photos from the Manhattan Beach Pier."

Tiare quickly left the table and unlocked her bike. She returned the lock to a waiter close by and left the scene. She wondered how Mic knew where to find her. She hoped that he wasn't anywhere close to her hotel. Halfway back to her room, she pulled over.

"Of course, my sister is meddling once more. She gave Mic the name of my hotel. Perhaps my sister was correct about Mark. I'm beginning to see his weaknesses, but she didn't have to interfere. I would have caught on to his excuses and self-absorbed needs, or better yet, narcissism and mother complex. There's a massive difference between the two men. Mic only is self-absorbed. Today was the first-time Mark's old charm and manipulation didn't work on me and the other man's calm reaction did. I'm surprised at my feelings. Who is the woman at the restaurant with Mic? Was she about some race business? Mic isn't dating anyone but me. Or is he? Did he manipulate his meeting to coincide with mine? If so, why? Mic said that he loved me. All guys say that."

Mic wrapped his meeting up and drove back to the hotel. He needed to talk to Tiare to squelch any other designs lover boy might have on his woman. There wasn't any Ivy League college in his background like the Mark guy, but he was intelligent enough to do the college round while also racing the tracks.

Mic groaned at his thoughts.

He knew he would have to explain to her honestly how he found her and why he used some of these profoundly opaque ideas at meeting her. She didn't seem excited to see him so soon. Her expression said it all. He was unbrilliant around her sometimes plus she looked a little mad. He wondered how mad?

Mic's plans were made solely for her benefit this weekend. He wanted to introduce her to his band of friends that evening. He also made other plans but might have to move those to some other time. Mic and his bodyguard walked toward the pier to find her. The old wooden pier was nine-hundred-twenty-feet long. Mic worried they missed her until he saw his woman. She was at the very end of the pier, of course.

11   Trent's Meeting with Sawyer

TRENT RUDY EASILY ditched the police tail following him by running through several hotel ramps and back alleys. Trent took the bus to and from the race track. Rudy swapped license plates with the hotel cleaning lady. Jim Michaels was unsuccessful planting a device on Rudy's rental car.

Trent kept nothing in his hotel room, carrying his small backpack style duffle bag in and out with him. The backpack was put in a locker in a gym across the street from the tracks. He knew an old friend who worked there who let him into the gym for free.

Later Trent Rudy drove to Kevin Sawyer's last known location which was a seedy motel where a person could pay by the week to get the cheapest of rates. This was the only way the motel could stay in business as the local stripper bar went out of business a couple of month's previous. The motel owners were desperate for money and started taking checks and credit cards. They didn't care if either were stolen. No one carried cash anymore, except the cops.

The main office's window was glass with metal bars and their new door was metal. They felt safe as a business. The rooms, however, were up-for-grabs to the mercenary gangs. Bullet holes were easily repaired as the motel owner's son was a painter. The daughter's husband ran a fumigation business to remove dead rats and termites. That's what the owners called the bodies that piled up on occasion. When the yellow tape came out from the police, the owners closed shop for three weeks and went to the sister's place in Florida. The motel was a win-win, booming business. The name of the motel was Ever Lasting.

Trent saw Sawyer's motorcycle in the parking lot. Reaching Sawyer's room door, he lightly knocked. There was no answer which was unusual. He looked over the balcony and there was no one around. He wiggled the cheap lock with a device and the door opened. The smell that came out of the crack made him step back. He took out his handkerchief. Wiping the door knob, he scrubbed any place he might have touched.

Trent knew the smell. There was something dead in the room. He wondered if the place contained mice or some other kind of rodent. But then, Sawyer was known to leave an uneaten hamburger in his room for three weeks. The smell wasn't exactly hamburger.

Putting the red handkerchief over his nose, he found Sawyer tied to a chair and he looked very dead. Trent looked at the man's clothes and the floor, but he didn't see any blood. A bullet would have made a hole and a mess. This kill couldn't have been a bullet. The man's face looked strange and puffy. The face was distorted. Trent almost touched the body when a fly landed on Sawyer and keeled over. There would be no touching. He figured more than a fumigation service would be required.

Trent quickly surveyed the room and unlocked the man's old briefcase. He took out his small notebook computer, charger, and set of keys. He didn't want to take the man's phone. He spied the blue envelope he had given him with the money. There was no money in the envelope.

"What did he do with my money? Eff, I'm never getting that loan back. But who killed him and why? Well, maybe they killed for the leftover money. There probably wasn't that much. This was like, maybe, a professional job? What in the world brought the man down?"

He checked the man's wallet, read the name, and was surprised the contents showed five hundred dollars still within the fold. That made even less sense other than this kill was clearly not a robbery. He didn't know what happened here with his friend. The man didn't deserve to die for being a hustler in the small change world. There were bigger fish out there. It was a kill that would bother him. He agreed with his mind that this kill was not done by your average local gang of thugs. He suddenly remembered what the police investigator, Derek, told him.

Trent knew he had to get out of this room and fast. Everlasting or immortality in this life might not be happening. Deader than a doornail came to mind. Things didn't work out for Sawyer in this dump. He worried about the name of this place. It was not a good omen. He picked up the five hundred dollars. Then he laid the money back down. Trent stared at the money. Was the money tainted? He sat down and waited. Soon, a fly walked over the money and flew away. The fly said, "Take the money." It was all right to stash the bills which he did in his back pocket.

Rudy drove his rental car a mile away, switched back the plates, and called the rental people to pick it up because the brakes sometimes stuck. He was going to find a different rental company. He canceled his hotel room. Walking back to the seedy motel, he waited until the maid went into a room and then he started Sawyer's motorcycle. He was running or crawling out of everyone's sights as fast as the motorcycle could take him. Trent kept hearing Derek Wright's words about snakes. The word resonated with the engine noise. He now believed his friend, Sawyer, was possibly poisoned.

XXXXXX

Trent drove toward Big Bear Lake, California. There would be lots of tourists this time of year. The location was close to San Bernardino where his mother lived. He could take Highway 18 to visit her. Remembering there was a driver who helped his mother on occasion with meals, he changed his mind. The mother called her son to let him know her driver was off to Cuba. Her driver's cabin was empty. This was the reason for a correction to his plans. The driver man wouldn't be using the cabin at Big Bear Lake anytime soon. He knew where the man kept his hidden key because his mother told him. She talked for hours about the driver, his cabin, small boat, and fishing rod. This was one time he listened. The driver kept his bar well-stocked and there were canned goods, too. The local store carried anything else required for a month or so. Trent just needed to buy milk, bread, hamburger, sausage, and eggs. The cabin was a gift. He would take it.

The drive would give him time to think and allow him the ability to disappear. He knew that he was afraid. The police detectives' interview and the death at the motel unnerved him.

"There is a hyper-intelligent snake woman and then the fake screwed-up copycats or snake wannabe-thugs."

Trent was questioning all his transactions. Who was who? He knew that he saw something but couldn't quite pull the information into his foggy brain. He felt powerless and feebleminded. Nothing was coming into his brain.

"Was the *something* to do with the red sport car, the yellow car parts, the woman in Miami, or her roommate?"

He stopped at a roadside trucker fueling station and purchased a newspaper to read. An idea hit him.

"I'm screwed unless the roommate is the missing key. Think, man. The roommate disappeared. The time of death and day when the other Hanson woman died were when I was at their location. Did the roommate see me and know about my investigation into Minnow Surf? Did she know the sports car was stolen originally? Who was Minnow and how did he connect?"

He was still confused. There was no way to reconstruct or understand the happening of events.

"Was the yellow sports car just a fluke? How did that car fall under this dirty business? There were just pieces floating around. How could a tiny part matter?"

His brain kept going around and round. Then there was Sawyer. He knew the man and what he was capable of hiring done. The man's anger toward the two race car drivers, Dan and Mic, was huge. The man wanted their world brought down.

"Sawyer mattered, somehow. He is another key."

Trent hoped things would blow over. He was running out of money and would need a job soon. There were always the forestry job openings, campgrounds, or boat launch ramps. He could even work for a resort, because he did that previously. He remembered there was a fishing boat and gear at the driver friend's cabin. The fishing stuff was in the storage garage. He would look at those items shortly. There was a gas pump at the local store. That made him smile. He would rather fish than chase women.

The longer the delay and as more days passed with no problems, the safer he would feel. However, he didn't understand the criminals at this level. Their network was extensive, making all federal and international agencies tracking them seem inferior. It was clear that soon Trent would feel nothing.

He would have had better luck volunteering as a cleanup worker on the next Russian spacecraft travelling to the International Space Station. The station was the only safe outpost to duck down out of sight of the bad guys, flying two hundred forty-eight miles from earth, eating up five miles per second. Or he would have been better off going with the motel owners to Miami. Except the way his luck was running, he would probably get hit by an asteroid getting there to either place.

Then there was always Mexico. Lots of people got lost there all the time. There were underground tunnels everywhere. Joining the drug cartel could have extended his life a couple of years or maybe the tequila and margaritas that did that. Then there were the senoritas that would have hid him. Yes, even Mexico would have been a better choice.

Either way, he made a bad decision to go to Big Bear Lake in California and then a worst decision to buy his bait at the Bait Shop. The shop was next to the store and fuel pump. Everyone went there. Someone was there and recognized him. The snake people love the woodlands. The dangerous snakes hide.

12 Manhattan Beach Pier

MIC AND HIS bodyguard strolled down to the end of the Manhattan Beach Pier. Mic finally saw Tiare and approached her.

"Don't you love the air here? It tastes like pure sea salt. There is no smell or feeling like it. Throw in a little rain and smog, and then it's perfect."

She stared at him.

"You must stop following me. I hate it."

"You don't waste time. Women want me to follow them. Most women want men to chase them. They've been doing the chase-scene for centuries."

Tiare wanted to club him. She continued looking off in the distance. Mic handled difficult women before except Tiare was even more so. He always told the boys at the track that he jumped at a challenge. Now was the time to put his money where his mouth was. She was a challenge.

"I thought we might have some easy conversation first."

"Easy. Is that what I am?"

"Oh, man, touchy again. I guess that I did mess up a little bit. And no, you're not easy at all. Let me explain. They changed my car slot on the track schedule and there I was with nothing to do until Tuesday. I didn't want to sit still. I thought why not visit my girl for a long weekend. My girl is pretty and a little crazy like someone I've never met before. You are enough to make a decent man do strange things. Nightlife and fun was rocking my brain. Besides, I wanted to surprise you."

She nodded, "You did surprise me a fourth time and somehow ruined my luncheon with an old friend. I should just give up eating out."

"I'm sorry about your luncheon. It did turn out a little strange. Your old boyfriend was a mess. A little soap and water would make a world of difference. Although, to be honest, I was glad to see him leave. Also, I wasn't appreciating his hands on you for one minute. He made me mad. It's a testosterone thing."

"Testosterone my foot. There was downright jealousy," said Tiare.

"You're right. There's the jealousy and then the other thing. I thought that we were clicking together in a relationship back in Michigan. A question does seem to arise. Can you explain why you didn't tell me where you were going for the weekend?"

Mic looked at her seriously because he had to ask her. Her disappearance was nagging at his brain. He thought they were close and in a bright, sexy new relationship.

Tiare sighed. "I didn't want to explain to you my plans. You would have objected. My friend wanted to discuss some idea he had. How was I to know he has separated again from his wife?"

Mic nodded, "I would have objected. The old boyfriend separated again? I get it now. The cave man thought he could waltz right back into your life. Now that's an abjectly thoughtless person who's tasteless, too."

Both were silent. Mic could see his bodyguard sweating and starring at people eating ice cream. He didn't' know what type of ice cream she even liked and here he was trying to lock her down. He needed to lighten up. Perhaps he was the only one thinking relationship.

"Would you like some ice cream? I saw a shop on the way to the pier. They make their own waffle cones. Let me guess which flavor. Is it strawberry? No, how about chocolate? Don't tell me that it's vanilla? You don't look like a vanilla girl."

Tiare finally laughed. "Cave man, really? Tasteless is what I was thinking."

"Are we still talking about the vanilla ice cream?"

Tiare turned to look directly at Mic. "Tasteless and vanilla are high on my avoidance list. The weather is hot. I could use something cool. I do like rainbow sherbet or sometimes lemon. They are like summer rain and yellow flowers."

"Rainbow and flowers work for me. I can picture you in yellow."

Mic saw a flicker of love in her eyes and held out his hand to her. He would take a small leak in the floodgate between them any time. It was just a matter of delay before things would give way. At least he was hoping they were on the right track.

"Let's go find the delectable cold shop and get out of the heat."

They were almost through with their cold frozen treats when Mic asked her out on a date.

"I have a friend who is a musician and plays the nightclubs when he is in the Los Angeles area. He plays just about any kind of music but likes pop-jazz best. The woman you saw with me at lunch today is his wife. Perhaps you have heard of them? They are Terrance and Michelle Reston or better known as the Terelle Triumphs. We can make it a dinner date with a little music and dancing later. How about it? I hope you are free this evening."

Tiare wasn't sure she wanted to be with Mic. She was still upset with him. She was more upset with Mark and her inability to dump the man in the past. She hesitated too long.

"Did, I forget to mention that my friend always allows me the opportunity to play electric guitars together with him on stage. We used to jam in the college dorm."

Tiare knew the music of the popular Terelle Triumphs and liked their sound. Seeing Mic play would be a bonus.

"I do like their music and I am tempted. If we go, I want an expensive dinner included in the deal with very red meat."

"You've got it. Can you be ready at six? We need to arrive early at the very, very expensive hotel restaurant for dinner?"

They reached the door of her room. Mic hoped she would invite him inside.

"Yes, I will be ready. See you later. I have a call that has appeared on my phone that I must answer."

Mic leaned over and kissed her. She tasted sweet like her rainbow cone.

"All right, I'll see you then. Six it is."

Mic and his bodyguard went to their room. Mic knew the call on her phone was more than likely the fool, Mark Draydon. He realized he hadn't exactly eradicated the man from Tiare's life.

13   Mic and the Musician Friend

PICKING UP TIARE, Mic drove to the hotel restaurant. They let the valet park the rental vehicle. After ordering their drinks, Mic turned to her, "You always look great. I don't know how a woman can have such a tiny suitcase and then look like a beauty contestant."

"It's called wonder fabric. The outfits disappear off the racks first because the fabric whispers to a woman that she doesn't even have to try. Looking good is the manufacturer's guarantee."

"Well, they nailed it with the yellow and coral combination. You look super amazing. All the men in this place turned their head when you stepped in the room."

Tiare smiled. She knew the stretchy dress was a killer.

They finished their filet mignon in browned mushroom sauce. They walked across the street to the nightclub and Mic introduced his friends to Tiare. The crowd filled the room and the music rolled. The band took a break and Terrance and Michelle Reston sat down with them.

"Well, I have thought about your discussion with my wife this afternoon. Here's the plan. We play our old gig-type music from college for the first song. Then I introduce Henri. I've brought in an elderly gentleman who is very good with a Tahitian mandolin which should add a nice element to your song. He has played with us in the past. You do your song. When everyone claps, and stands up, my security people will walk with you to your vehicle."

"Thanks for bringing in the mandolin guy. What if they don't clap and stand up? It's been a long time since I performed."

"Are you kidding me? You perform every day in that race-cat object of yours unless you're sleeping at the wheel?

Terrance slapped Mic on the back. "Don't worry. We'll cover for you and play real loud."

Mic relaxed. It was like old times.

Tiare looked at Mic, "You sing?"

"I used to a long time ago. Singing helped pay for my college classes."

Both men went to the stage and the awaiting band. Mic and Terrance played their first set. The audience clapped and stood up.

"See, I told you they would do that."

Then it was Mic's turn to sing. Terrance bowed to his audience once more. He turned, bowed to Mic, and handed him the microphone.

"Go grab some glory so you can impress your nice date. Oh, and knock out those other ladies with your rock-soul charm."

Terrance brought out a high bar stool for Mic and his wife brought out the steel guitar. She positioned her hands to pluck the strings. Mic sat down with the electric guitar sitting low on his hips. He plucked a few strings and talked to his friendly audience.

"I have a song that I've written which is new. I've rehearsed it mentally with a music background tape from my friend. Let me tell you that this is the first time with a live audience. By the way, we will record this one for a special friend. The beauty of a first time is that if I stumble a little, you won't know it or if you realize it, you will forgive me."

Mic looked at Tiare. His audience laughed. They would forgive him.

"Some of the phrases repeat and if you want to join in, please go ahead. I'll give you a signal like so."

He did a motion with one hand. It was a hand gesture the flagman made in the old days.

"The song is a Caribbean and drum sound. The story is about a man struggling in his quest to find his love."

Terrance picked up the bongo drums and said, "Ready, one, and two, and three."

Mic began the beautiful fast-paced rhythm with an introduction and then started his song. He smiled at Tiare because he wrote the song for her and she would soon know it.

"Color me gone, gone, gone.
She gets my engine rocking and rolling.
Heck, I can't even remember her name.
But you know her, yes, you do.

She swings in perfect motion on her stiletto shoes.
Her red-honeyed hair lights night into a smoldering fire.

Oh, yeah, I'm so gone, gone, gone.
She's an illusion, creating confusion with
miracle kisses.
You can find her eating rainbow sherbet on a
Manhattan Pier.
She tastes like heavenly ecstasy which
shouldn't be missed."

Mic kept strumming and looked at Tiare and she
was smiling so he went into the song further.

"Color me gone, gone, gone.
She gets my engine rocking and rolling.
Heck, I can't even remember her name.
But you know her, yes, you do.

There isn't a tiara as beautiful as her image.
She's a diamond whose smile makes a man
rise.
Oh, yeah, I'm so gone, gone, gone.
She's a fragrant flower worth traversing a
thousand miles.
One can find her on a pretty green Polynesian
isle.
In the land of sweet dreams lies paradise."

Mic motioned to the audience that is where it
was their turn to join him.

"Color me gone, gone, gone.
She gets my engine rocking and rolling.
Heck, I can't even remember her name.
But you know her, yes, you do.

She reigns, wearing a Ti-leaf headdress made
with feather art.
The woman separates the lonely from a young
man's heart.
Oh, yeah, I'm so gone, gone, gone.
Her eyes brighten Hollywood with her magic
glitter.
Local boys start drinking kickass rum with
bitters.
It's a wonder anyone's standing and not
woefully stoned."

Mic strummed a little more. He was enjoying
himself. Tiare and the audience were, too. His friend
nodded that the song was working.

"Color me gone, gone, gone.
She gets my engine rocking and rolling.
Heck, I can't even remember her name.
But you know her, yes, you do.

She's the hauntingly beautiful one lying on a
rope hammock
Her tanned body has flawless bones and
molten lips of sugar.
Oh, yeah, I'm so gone, gone, gone.
Sex on shifting white sand are memories that
certainly stick.
Hot and salty ocean breezes sweetly caress
her.
Seagulls entertain, performing their taunting
tricks.

Color me gone, gone, gone.

She gets my engine rocking and rolling.
Heck, I can't even remember her name.
But you know her, yes, you do.

You can find her on a swaying palm tree
island.
She's dancing in the distance to a musical
tune.
Oh, yeah, I'm so gone, gone, gone.
Hips are swinging in a silk pareo, enticing
more than the sky.
Let me lie low, work the last lap, hanging tight
to the rail.
Will I capture a slide-in show to match her
man-scale?"

Mic motioned to his audience and stood up. He
moved and did a little dance while serenading the
women at the front tables. All the women stood up.
Tiare and his bodyguard stood up as did the rest of his
audience because they knew the song was almost over.
Tiare was moved by his love song. He could have quit
right there. He won her heart. Mic raised his hand to
Terrance to pick up the beat a little.

"Color me gone, gone, gone.
She gets my engine rocking and rolling.
Heck, I can't even remember her name.
But you know her, yes, you do.

Start the syncopation. Ask her questions that
rhyme. Is there a caution flag? Such a drag.
Or is her hand punching the green light sign?"

Mic was strolling and moving back toward Tiare. His voice rose louder, and he put his soul into the song. His rock and roll charm were laid down. Terrance was grinning. The guy still had the stuff.

"Oh, yeah, I'm so gone, gone, gone.
You change my world and make me stronger.
No track in the world is as hard to win as you.
Here I am, one foot in front of the other,
stepping closer.

Oh, yeah, I'm so gone, gone, gone.
I could repeat this melancholy song, but I don't want to.
I've got to catch you before the evening's through.
Heaven help make my dreams come true.
Whoo, Hooo, Hooo."

Mic pointed at Tiare and blew her a kiss.

"Color me yours. I'm falling into your arms.
E Ku'u Aloha, my sweet believable ray.
Take my hand, our love's awakening.
There's no need to rewind the glorious day.
Roll down the back stretch, miles we're gaining.
Oh, heck, yeah, we'll raise off-the-wall times.
I'm calling your name, love, and do remember just fine.

Oh, yeah, I'm so gone, gone, gone.

My focused heart sees a checkered spectrum.
Hold on tight now. Paradise is across the
finish line.
Let's end this song.
Color us—so long, long gone!
And one more time.
Whoo…Hooo…Hooooo."

Mic raised the guitar high in the air. Moving the stool out of the way, he handed the guitar and microphone back to his friend, Terrance. He shook hands with the mandolin player.

He bowed to Terrance and his audience. Next, he hugged his dear friend and his wife. The audience stood up and cheered loudly.

Mic accepted their thanks and returned the words to them, "Mahalo."

He waved to the group of ladies in the front and bowed one last time. They wanted to go to the tropical swaying beach or anywhere else with just him. The women wanted someone to call them my love in any kind of language. They would go back home and call their travel person to get them and their husband on the next flight to somewhere else, anything tropical.

Mic wanted to kiss a smiling Tiare, but he took Tiare's arm quickly with his bodyguard in toe and exited the building. One of the people in the audience was a race car fan and put the words he sang together. He recognized Mic as his favorite racer. He called out Mic's full name.

"It's Mic Palla everyone, the popular race car driver."

Mic's identity was known and now was the time to run to their vehicle to avoid the deluge of people wanting his autograph. His friend's bodyguard helped them escape for the night. The news media weren't there. Mic developed other plans for their evening. The timing of everything would work in his favor.

Mic received a text on his cell phone that the champagne and bouquet of gardenias were delivered. He felt the diamond bracelet in his pocket. This was going to be a perfect night. He did know how to manipulate and use his known skills and tricks. Ditching an annoying competitor was part of the game.

"Where there's smoke, a little fire always helps."

The Ivy League boyfriend was getting bumped out of the race.

14   Dead Body & Plan

THE POLICE NOTIFIED Derek of the dead body which was identified as Kevin Sawyer. He was murdered by what they feared might be a poisonous substance. Forensics would identify the kill as strangulation. But first the man was beaten in the face.

The kill was not snake poison. The Dendroaspis polylepis or black mamba snake poison was nowhere in the man or on the premises. The snake, among the fastest of the venomous creatures, delivers from its inky black mouth, a highly potent mixture of toxins which hit the central nervous system and muscles such as the heart. Once the poison is delivered, a person will die unless they receive the anti-venom.

Mr. Sawyer didn't know his time was up. This man died of lack of oxygen.

They checked his bank accounts and found a check from Trent Rudy for fifty thousand dollars. Then funds were withdrawn in two separate transactions of twenty-five thousand dollars each within the last month. The search was placed to locate Mr. Rudy again for questioning and potential arrest.

A cleaning lady saw a woman whom she thought might be a man on the upper balcony near Mr. Sawyer's room. The police asked her if she could come down to the station to look at mug shots. Suddenly, she had no clue who or what the person was that she saw. Her car license plate was missing. The woman's memory suddenly got smart and she played dumb. The cleaning lady couldn't miss a whole day's work to help police. Plus, she didn't want any murderers messing with her. A person never knew what creeps could enter their world. She could become a missing person. Her name wasn't Lucy for anything. Lucy played things smart and watched lots of soap opera and mystery shows. The cleaning lady would imitate her idols.

The police were frustrated. Derek worried, "What were the two payments regarding? This man was found in a seedy motel and once lived in a mansion. Was the first money some loan possibly from Mr. Rudy?" Derek had an edgy feeling more trouble was on the horizon. He told Jim and Tami about the additional details. He asked Jim to watch their race car drivers and talk with them again about the two men in question.

Tami informed him that Mic and Tiare were at Manhattan Beach for the weekend. Derek called Jess and told her about his plan. Jess contacted Rhonda and invited them to dinner aboard the yacht in their slip at San Diego pier.

She left a message for Tiare, inviting her, Mic, and his bodyguard to dinner also to see their yacht. Tiare missed their last party in Miami because she was in school. The Wrights owed her dinner.

Jess's friend heard Mic sing to Tiare at the nightclub. She told Jess the guy was good in all the hunk categories. The women in her group of friends loved the guy at the hotel nightclub and wanted him to sing again. Jess thanked her friend for the call. Now, she was extremely curious about Mic, the race car driver, and performer.

The plan was to get Mic comfortable around the Wrights for a relaxing Sunday dinner among friends.

Derek would set up a later meeting to talk with Mic. Rhonda would be present for questions about the interviews she did with his ex-wives. Derek also wanted to obtain more information from Mic soon regarding his time with Trent Rudy and Kevin Sawyer.

The police and Derek felt the accidents at the track were hits possibly purchased by Mr. Sawyer or Mr. Rudy. The last money was pulled out of the bank account only three days earlier. There was another opportunity that the final hit wasn't yet complete.

They thought the track would be the location. The bomb experts were contacted. Mamba snake anti-venom would be available for the medical people at the track via an undercover doctor just in case. The police drill would happen because they knew no clues as to what might happen next.

Anything could happen.

15   Yacht Dinner Party

RHONDA AND SKID arrived first and visited with the Wright children. Mic, Tiare, and his bodyguard arrived at their dock and walked up the high-end carbon fiber gangway. Tiare held onto the railing to support her body in stilettos. The gangway slid into the inside of the yacht when not in use. Mic noticed the yacht's name was on the gangway which contained LED lights.

He read the name Silver Zephyr on the gangway and then he noticed the helicopter with varying bands of gray with the initials SZ that faded into a white ocean wave.

"These friends of yours travel in style. This yacht looks like a custom job. I bet this thing flies over the water."

Tiare laughed, "Yes, it definitely is super custom-loaded and the thing does go fast especially since Derek upgraded the engines."

"Power is good. He's my kind of man then. Is that a possible gun on the helicopter?"

"What do you think? He works with the police," mentioned Tiare.

Mic noticed the security crew on board the yacht. He knew they were packing guns. He was impressed.

"How long is the Wright's yacht?"

"Oh, I believe about one-hundred-sixty-feet long by maybe twenty-eight feet wide. The yacht has five staterooms besides the master bedroom. There also is a sub on the ship."

Mic laughed. "This is a mega, smoking hot, super yacht, fully loaded, and holds a helicopter and sub. Are there any other guns and toys on board?"

"Yes, many of each one and they are definitely smoking hot."

Derek met them at the top of the gangway with a tray of champagne in their SZ etched tall glasses.

"Welcome aboard. Have a quick prelude drink and meet my beautiful wife, Jess. Then I'll take you on a tour of the yacht. Our crew will ready her for takeoff. We'll be cruising during further cocktails and our dinner. Hi, sweetheart, it's so nice to see you."

Derek bent down and let Tiare hug and kiss him.

"Hi, to you, too, I've missed your company. By the way, this is a very nice yacht. Tami told me all about it."

Mic shook Derek's hand. He welcomed and motioned him to step aboard. Mic accepted the extended glass of champagne. He introduced his bodyguard whose eyes were still glazed-over regarding the yacht. Mic laughed.

"I will second that on the smoking yacht and I'm interested in what's on your heli-pad."

Derek joined him in the laugh. He was pleased his guests liked the yacht and they hadn't even seen the rest of ship. He knew Jess would be pleased as well. She loved their yacht.

The group met back in the dining room for dinner. The chef's staff served a layered, light mixed green salad with tomato lemon vinaigrette. The main meal was a tiered affair with a round layer of garlic scalloped potatoes, filet mignon, cooked and peeled crab with a small lobster tail on top. The plate contained horseradish sauce and a twirl of seafood sauce matching the SZ logo shape. Mic wondered what was on the menu for dessert. There was dark chocolate mousse with white chocolate on top. The sweet wafer was in a helicopter shape and tasted of vanilla butter.

The conversation turned to the music Mic performed at the nightclub. Jess told Mic that she would like to hear the video tape that was made. If he was good enough, he might want to see if Wade Brookston wanted to purchase the lyrics. Rhonda had written the song, Golden Girl, and a couple others for Wade. Plus, they saw Wade occasionally perform with their son, Justin, when he was touring in the area.

Mic was impressed with Rhonda, the woman he knew as Glamour. She was part of an amazing group of intelligent women that crossed his world. He wondered if she told her husband the name he called her. He winked at Rhonda when Skid wasn't looking. Then he talked with Justin the rest of the dinner about his music.

Jess noticed the seventy-five-thousand-dollar diamond bracelet on Tiare's right arm. Jess knew her diamonds, and she acknowledged that Mic bought the best. He probably hadn't told Tiare the price. The price for that quality of diamonds was outrageous. The man loved her outrageously. His current state of divorce or sin-focused poisoner on the loose didn't matter.

Jess would fix Tiare's lack of diamond knowledge and inform her sister, Tami, of the expensive present. She hoped that information would lead to more visits by the two to their yacht. She liked the young man, Mic. He could add so much fun to their parties. Mic probably knew a thousand stories to tell about the race track. She wanted to see more of him in Tiare's life, instead of boring Mark Draydon. Jess wasn't too keen about the old boyfriend.

Then, there was the other problem. Someone wanted to bring Mic down. Jess could feel his pain over that issue. Mic hid his feelings well. He hid his thoughts from Tiare on the potential murderer that entered his life. Jess would give him points for bravery. She liked knights. Mic was one of them. She saw Tiare who was also brilliant in her field. The pair were a good match and Tiare was relentless. Jess had seen qualities in the child when she was young and was glad. The mix of the two was a good combination.

Currently, there was stress and duress in their lives. Mark Draydon was a nit. Jess would help. This was important. There was much work to do. She would focus on ways to help Derek in this game of trickery. Trouble was on the horizon. She was good at mysterious. She saw through the criminals' veils of wickedness.

Vengeance was the screwball con artist mixed into the life of normal people. There was some sort of vengeance brewing in the atmosphere. Forbidden stuff would enter the fray. She wondered about whose stuff was forbidden. Was it the law or self-imposed something? There, she said the words. *There was something brewing, with a vengeance.*

Derek saw Jess plotting in her mind. She saw the stumbling love happening between Tiare and Mic. Jess felt their pain. She didn't want them to miss true love. Derek missed her last thoughts. Her husband always missed things with his wife. Finding out her computer code only helped when she wanted him to know what was there. She kept a second code, just to be on the safe side. Someday, Jess would need to tell her husband. Now was not a good time. It wasn't that she didn't trust her husband. She did. The problem was the bad people that invaded their lives. Jess created an alternate way to communicate to her husband if need be. Jess would use the new code in their future. It would be her only line of defense. It would help save everything. That is everything that was important.

Jess raised her glass to her husband because he represented her true love, and she saluted him. Derek knew she covered this evening dinner superbly. Derek chuckled even more. Mic didn't have a clue what was going to hit him with Jess on his side. Jess knew she would move heaven and earth for one of her own. Tiare was part of their female group of women-power.

Derek raised his glass to his wife and smiled. He knew their female women-power was a good happening. He accepted the fact they were a powerful force only women understood. If their group helped him, he was always glad. Derek knew not to question his wife about her plans. Jess would only share them if things were critical. She planned her dinners and their life well. His wife gained valuable insight.

Derek crunched loudly on his helicopter cookie to let her know he was appreciative of her efforts. His wife would include him on anything important or, so he thought. He suddenly wished Dean Crain were there. Dean had somehow figured out his wife. Derek was currently getting there.

Jess smiled back with a twinkle in her eyes which was not missed by anyone at their table. Derek would have to wait until later to hear her plan. He knew there would be no mistakes in her plan. His woman always brewed a great one.

The men talked about helicopters during dessert and Mic liked Skid. They were about the same age. Both men liked danger, one race cars and the other one, the strange wild creatures of the deep. Mic wasn't sure he could do the tango with sharks and octopus. They were for eating in a gourmet restaurant. Race cars and women were his forte.

Mic turned to Jess.

"Thank you for the lovely dinner and lively guests on your super yacht. This visit has been an absolute pleasure and meeting you. I'll seriously think about the song being published."

He felt Jess was one of those powerful and beautiful women in his song. He developed a new respect for Derek. The man was very gone on his very talented wife. Mic knew how that felt. Then he looked at Tiare and was glad she was having a good time. The dinner was a good break for both. He could hardly wait to get her alone. She was spinning his world. He didn't care about his upcoming race. It had been a long time since he felt that way. The races were everything. This was a new experience.

Jess noticed the way the two young lovers glanced at each other. She was pleased. There were romantic messages flying across the table during dinner.

Jess told Mic that he must come back another time to meet their daughter, Sami, and Skid's daughter, Maggie. They were staying for the weekend with Jim's wife who was taking the girls shopping.

Derek shook hands with the men and hugged Tiare again.

"Good night. Take care of our boy."

"I will," responded Tiare. "I've got my gun, knife, and handcuffs ready. Then there are always the karate moves or ropes."

Derek looked at her. "Just use them on any of your next suspects. Currently, Mic is not a suspect."

Tiare laughed.

Derek shook his head. "I don't want to go there tonight with the ropes. I've heard about your stunt from your sister."

"She's always been a tattle-tale but in a good way."

Mic saw them laughing and wondered what the secret was between them.

The young lovers and bodyguard excused themselves and departed the yacht at ten thirty in the evening. Derek's security people made sure they made it back to their rental vehicle in the lighted parking lot.

16   Preparation for the Race

MIC AND TIARE returned Monday to the track. Mic planned one final round of timed runs and then he would know his placement in the race. His other team players received good slots for Friday's race. Wednesday and Thursday were completely booked on his schedule with events that he must attend for his sponsors and the meet-and-greets scheduled with race fans.

Mic kissed a sleepy Tiare, got dressed, and drove with his bodyguard to the tracks. He saw Dan approaching. Mic didn't want to talk with the man this morning.

"I'm going to keep you behind me for this race. You can eat my dust permanently."

Mic wasn't going to let the man get to him this morning. The day was too early, and he saw some officials watching.

"Did Tiare see that Draydon guy or was she with you all weekend?"

Mic squinted and wondered which one of his crew told Dan where he went.

"Look, pal, the lady makes her own decisions. You will need to check her private rules on men with her. I don't need to ball and chain any of my women anymore. They flock around me willingly, as you well know."

"Too bad the inner field isn't manure which is your next parking spot if she was with you."

"Suit yourself, but your plan sounds mighty reckless to me."

Mic looked at dark and angry eyes. He saw Jim Michaels approaching and was glad that this conversation would end.

"Hello, Mic, hope you had a nice weekend. I hear you visited some friends of mine," mentioned Jim.

Dan turned abruptly and walked away bumping Jim aside.

"I hope he's not driving today. The man looks a little sour."

"Yes, he has one more timed run and probably will push it too far. Maybe both tires will fall off."

Jim looked at Mic. "I think you need to keep those thoughts to yourself."

Mic looked at the disappearing race car driver. "Yeah, I can do that, because I'm not desperate. I already won the important, alluring woman."

Jim shook his head. This gig was tough being around so much male testosterone in such small territory. He thought they should make the tracks three times longer and five miles wider to allow the steam to tamp down the dust and stop the mud from flying. Maybe it would be a good idea to put a lake in the middle. Also, some hoses would be good to control the fire and smoke. Next, Jim thought about the alligators that invaded golf courses in Florida.

"Alligators in a lake in Florida could be a problem."

"What are you talking about, Jim."

"Oh, just lunch. Fried would be good, alligator that is."

Mic said, "Come on, I'll buy you coffee, black, sinfully dark, right? Maybe grab some fat chocolate chip cookies. The track deli counter doesn't offer alligator, but they do sell sour gummy worms. We have complained because the kids throw them on the tracks. Take a sour driver and sticky sour gummy worms sticking to your wheels. It's a nightmare slowdown."

"That's correct. Then there's the peanuts. Peanuts are good. I hate those popcorn boxes and the popcorn balls. They are just as bad as the gummy worms on the tracks. If they banned the food, probably no one would show up for the race."

Now it was Mic's turn to laugh. He was going to have a good run. Tiare loved his song this weekend. He sung the song to her in private. He only got half way through the song and was forced to stop. He remembered which part of the song and exactly when she fell into his arms.

Mic was at the counter. "Coffee, black, and none of that latte crap." He winked at the pretty coed in the coffee area.

"Aren't women wonderful?"

"You remind me of someone, and I agree."

Jim hoped there were no more poison-laced lattes. He was still thinking about alligators and snakes. He wasn't sure which one was scarier. "Did they eat worms? More than likely."

Later, Mic disappeared in the evening with Tiare. In their room, he wore his blue cotton underwear and sang again to her. This was a new song. He threw the lampshade toward the garbage can and used the lamp as his guitar. Tiare laughed even harder when the lamp wire caught on his shorts. He had to eventually take them off because they were so ensnared. The underwear landed near the shade and garbage. He didn't care, all he wanted was her in his lair. It was a wonderful evening for the two lovers.

Mic came out of his fun world to arise and watch the morning sunshine. He felt amazingly great and went back to the track. He was brought back into the current conversation with Jim.

"Can you fry a snake?" asked Jim.

Mic didn't scare too easily and said, "Sure, fried snake is a delicacy. All you need is a little fire and smoke, possibly a bottle of ketchup, too. The meal might taste good with pork bacon. Are we snake-hunting this morning? I believe I just ran into one earlier. Or was that an alligator? No, maybe the tadpole turned into a frog which got eaten by a snake who crossed an alligator in Florida. There we are: *alligator wins until he crosses the road. The road is anyone's game.* Now there's food for thought."

Mic was evidently gone in the head this morning thought Jim. He, sort of, followed the story. He wondered how Dan fit in the roadway with the alligator.

"I didn't hear you say that. Nope, we haven't talked at all. Thanks for the dark coffee."

Jim went to find more rational conversation with calm, alluring women by the names of Tami and Tiare. Rhonda had warned Jim about Mic. Rhonda didn't know half the depths of competitive moves this race car driver could pass out. Jim wouldn't want to meet Mic on a race track. Suddenly, he felt sorry for Dan. Then he thought better of it. Dan could be scary, too.

"May the better man always win," said Jim. Obviously, the show would be interesting the longer a person hung around.

"Yes, siree. Today's another wonderful day at the race track."

17   Charity Runs

DEREK AND RHONDA arrived later in the week. They came to watch the race scheduled for the next day and planned to talk to Mic and Dan afterwards. They met Jim, Tami, and Tiare in the reserved conference room.

Derek said, "I forgot how noisy the race track was from the people, the smell of tires, hot engines, beer, and hotdogs."

Jim chuckled because he became used to the noise. "We'll go up to the enclosed seats in a little bit to watch some of the donation guests do their drive on the tracks. The T-shirt shops were extremely busy this morning with the fans wanting to purchase their special shirt. The crowd was keeping the police busy."

"They are having some of the teams test a new car on the tracks which should be interesting today," mentioned Tami.

"Yes, both Dan and Mic's teams will be in the test run. The crew chiefs have been hyping up the event to the media. That's why the campgrounds are full of people already," said Tiare.

"The place should be quieter for us in the upper enclosed deck today and tomorrow. Thanks, Jim, for coordinating the reservation."

Tami said, "All our people will be in place for the main race tomorrow and there will be extra Security teams everywhere. The police will have motorcycles in case we have a runner. There also will be barricades in certain places to restrict the traffic flow."

Derek was frowning. "I didn't know they were doing a test run today. Is that the new car with the lowered downforce? The race should be an interesting show with the drivers trying their passes. I hear the driver needs to be more skilled. That's probably why Dan and Mic are in the event. What time today is the test run?"

Jim looked at his schedule of events. "The schedule shows three thirty in the afternoon."

"Good, because we should have the Cortez brothers here by then and some of our crew from San Francisco."

"Derek, are you worried we might have the wrong event scheduled to catch the villain?"

"Yes, I'm getting strange vibes about the test run. I think we should all be prepared for the later race."

The charity event was over. The Cortez brothers checked in with Derek. He asked them if they were carrying.

"We're both packing and have some special military flare guns. Tami got us through Security," said Cortez.

Derek looked askance at Cortez. "Why do we need these heavy-duty flare guns? Maybe sling shots would be better."

"Hey, I'm really good with sling shots. I'm a perfect shooter. However, there's the snare rifle which worked great to bring down a drone. They are better than grenade launchers which leave too much of a mess. The mess from those launchers can look like a race track concession stand after a popcorn maker blew. We ditched the snare rifle. Plus, we didn't think Security would let us through with the snare rifle, because the gun was too dangerous."

"Really, and why is that?"

"We couldn't find a replacement cord that fit the antique rifle, so we tried out a different cord. We were changing the rifle into our own snare version. My brother and I were even thinking about writing up a patent. We set up a test."

Jim screwed up his face. "How old was this antique rifle?"

"Real old. In the test, we almost captured a prairie dog with the homemade snare rifle. Then, the cord wrapped around a rabbit in our neighbor's yard. We didn't know it was a pet. Tami thought we should have been able to figure that out by its huge size. It probably was the little wire inside the cord that was the problem. Anyway, the neighbor came stomping over to us. We apologized and offered to get him a new rabbit or we could send him a year's worth of fish. He demanded a year's worth of fish and then broke the rifle. He told us that was the only way to make things square again. We only paid twenty-five dollars for the rifle, so we were okay. Unfortunately, the rabbit didn't make it, and the owner really didn't care. Therefore, we're only going to give him the day-old fish from our restaurant."

Jim was standing next to Derek and started laughing. "I didn't know you had prairie dogs in Florida?" Jim was thinking day-old fish wasn't good enough.

Cortez laughed, "Yes, they are not native to Miami but there's a tribe of them around the airport where my brother lives. We looked the rodents up one day and we think they are the black-tailed ones. See, there was the second problem, the rabbit was black. Who buys their kid a black bunny for Easter? Like no one that I know on this planet. They might buy a white bunny with spots but not all black. Everyone knows you can't use the colored Easter egg dye on black fur. It doesn't show up too well."

Cortez's brother intervened. "Evidently, the rabbit liked the prairie dogs which we thought was a little odd. The bunny would follow them and chase around. The black bunny ran into a little bit of trouble trying to fit into their hole, and then he got stuck. That's how we caught him in the tail, and the darn thing wrapped the cord around tighter than a sheep left on a line. You know that you shouldn't tie up sheep because they get scared and become a twirling top. Well, neither should you try to ensnare a pet rabbit."

"We were the ones that felt bad. If it had been a local rabbit, that would have been a different story. Wild rabbit makes good fish bait. The meat is tougher than a worm and you can keep it in the water on your hook for a long time. Although sharks do hit the line right away. Frankly, it was a learning lesson about how not to use a snare rifle around pets," said Cortez.

Jim smiled, very much liking the conversation and ingenuity of the Miami brothers. Being around them was always entertaining. They made things work, albeit it was haphazard sometimes.

"Ok, boys, let's get in our selected locations. I heard the announcer, and I see the race cars on the track getting into position. Keep your flare guns close but also covered. We don't want to scare the crowd."

"Amen, to that."

18   Test Run Race

THE CARS WERE going to do twenty-five laps for the Specialty Test Run Race of the new cars. They were only going to run six cars for the race because that's all the company gave the speedway to test. The drivers were excited to be chosen. They knew each other well as competitors and were usually in the top twenty-five percent of winners. The drivers were shown a video taken inside the car on the track and read the spec sheet. They could inspect their car with their pit crew for a half hour before the race.

Tiare met Mic on the inner last gate to his pit area. She saw his car and kissed him. "Run like a panther, my love." She danced away from him.

"Oh, yeah, this was going to be super good."

The drivers were getting ready to enter their vehicles in their drawn positions. Mic liked his black race car and his number three. He looked over at Dan who mouthed the words, "Cow Shit."

Mic looked up at the sky and refrained from giving Dan the finger because there were too many cameras. Suddenly, he had a thought. He mouthed the words, "Panther Piss."

Dan frowned because he didn't know what Mic was trying to say. It didn't matter. They must get buckled in. Both men were so ready.

Secure in their vehicles with their helmets adjusted and pads in place for safety, the drivers were ready for the green. The engines roared with a humming sound and smoke clouded the air as they took off. The crowd roared. All the drivers drove fast and were pushing the cars to the limit. They were on the last lap and Mic liked the new design of his vehicle. The machine was quick to his response and he could sneak around a car into the space ahead.

Mic was leading the pack and the third driver, Crayman, snuck around both men. Then Mic shot past Crayman into the lead. Dan was on Crayman's tail and made his move capturing the second-place slot. Dan couldn't get around Mic. The reason for this was that Mic learned fast and became one with his black panther-cat car. He was quick to pounce and release in a game of tease. That pissed Dan off.

Derek looked in his binoculars and saw the blue-sky colored object.

"The object's a darn drone and expensive, too. He spoke into his microphone. "Cortez, go after the blue drone at two o'clock."

"We're on it."

Cortez took his cotton candy on the stick and held it close to the flare gun as a piece of camouflage. He would follow Derek's order. A brown-haired lady coming down the bleacher, cheap-seat area, bumped into him. The cotton candy tilted into the direct line of the extended barrel. He closely aligned up the special sight they found for the gun to the drone. The brass sight was purchased at an antique store. He put the sight directly on the drone nose. The sight was slightly bent and sawed off a little which made it work much better. Pulling the trigger, the flare zipped right through the cotton candy. The pieces of pink stickiness landed all over the back of the woman's hair. The flare gun sizzled from the pink cloud and the surrounding area smelled of burnt marshmallow with a hint of cherry smell.

"Drone going down, falling like a dizzy merry-go-round. I see pieces, oh, crap, it hit the top of Dan's car."

"Is that the barrel of a demon gun on that crazy busted drone?" said Cortez's brother as he lowered his binoculars.

Derek responded. "Yes, we're asking them to check out Dan and the vehicle. We need to keep people away from the second car."

Cortez wasn't looking at the screaming woman in front of him but was watching where the drone fell. He wished that he pulled the trigger sooner but had to readjust his sight on the drone. It took him only two seconds, but there was enough time for the drone to fire. Cortez's hit to destroy the drone was a perfect one. His brother nodded.

"You win again. That's two weeks in a row that I have to buy beer."

Cortez coughed, "Don't worry, I have plenty of money today. We can dunk our hot dogs in the beer and eat real fast to see who wins, but then you always win. Let's relax and grab three of those dogs before they close because I'm suddenly hungry. Then we can turn in our report."

Mic just crossed the finish line when the yellow caution light turned on. Dan was frowning, and something hard hit his windshield breaking his thoughts and caused him to overcorrect the wheel. Dan rammed his car into the fourth car that was trying to get past him. Both cars went into a spin causing the other cars behind them to scramble to avoid the whirling vehicles.

A half second later, Cortez's flare hit the drone and blew it up into fiery pieces which also landed on the track making the cars skate and lift. Now the last two cars were in trouble bumping into the rubberized walls.

The body of the drone landed on the hood of Dan's car in a hot heap sending sparks into the engine that caught fire.

Emergency vehicles were flying out of their waiting positions moving toward the two-stalled and mangled vehicles. Derek and his teams were trying to get through the crowd, who were standing up to see the show. It would take them awhile to reach the track.

Mic saw the mess as he turned the curve to enter his pit area and kept going around the track. Stopping his vehicle, he jumped out of the race car and ran across the track to check on Dan.

As he arrived, they were pulling him out of the vehicle and dousing his suit with flame retardant.

"Are you all right, Dan?"

Dan looked at Mic, "Hell-of-a-test run. I was dreaming and counting sheep. Next thing, I thought I saw my dead grandmother. She was shaking a cotton candy stick at me while knitting. It was scary as hell. I just hope that I'm in one piece and my underwear still fits."

Mic hugged him. "I'll lend you some of mine."

"What did you call me before this ratchet show started."

"Panther Piss."

"Is that jungle voodoo words cause look at this race car and all the junk," laughed Dan. "Something hit my car. I felt pain. What the heck is that on top my hood?"

"Don't know, but I'm sure we'll find out."

Dan grunted. "Whew, here come the medics to check me out. They ought to check the car first." He thought he was in shock because he fainted. The medics caught him and found he caught a bullet near his hip area once he was in the ambulance. They were amazed he could walk or talk. They figured the adrenaline worked overtime. The police were told as was Derek who grabbed Rhonda and headed in the direction of the hospital. He put his temporary light on the rental vehicle to clear the road.

Tiare went down to Mic's pit area and waited for him to return. Tami and Jim would stay with the police on the track to study the debris. The manufacturer of the test race cars looked a little bit upset. The speedway owners were easing him and his entourage into the awaiting conference room. Beer was ordered from the concession area. Beer always worked in stressful situations. The peanuts and popcorn were brought into the room, too. The woman with the sticky hair was talking to the manager about a refund on her tickets and concessions. She brought six people with her.

The end of the test race was close in time to the track closing which was a good thing. Security and Derek's other teams helped move everyone out of the stadium. There would be an investigation and it was questionable whether the race would take place the next day. The officials were pushing the police to make their investigation roll a little faster.

Rhonda told Derek that he owed Cortez a cotton candy. Derek told her to buy him a slingshot as well as a joke. The slingshot was to replace the snare rifle.

"Write on the wood, Perfect Shooter".

19   Snake Woman's Tracker

THE REAL TRACKER person located the Miami dead girl's roommate. The roommate was alive and was seen with Matin Domingo's former lawyer. The police were looking for him for questioning. The lawyer's name was Ed Burrows. The real tracker followed them to an off-shore bank and watched them come out with a large duffel bag. She turned to her partner.

"I'm sure there isn't newspaper in that bag. It most certainly is part of Domingo's illegal money from drugs and gun running. Let's check their room tonight while they are in the hotel lobby eating dinner. First, I need to contact Max Lewis, the Snake woman's counterpart, to inform them of the two persons' whereabouts."

Max told the Tracker to stay on the group who were obviously up to no good. Their worry was that the roommate and lawyer were setting up shop somewhere else, luring clients into their schemes and using the Snake woman's calling card. They heard about some poisonings in California and other hit jobs.

Tracker contacted Max who was waiting.

"Yes, the bag contains over twenty million. Do you want me to remove it?"

"No, let's let things ride. Keep following them. We saw her tattoo in your photo. Our thinking is that she killed her roommate, Coral Hanson, and others. The man and her have run two con games. First is the setup attempt at murder and they receive the initial installment of money. Attempts are made so they look sincere at murder and they don't get caught. They hire others for those smaller jobs. Then they hit the person for more money. If there are limited funds, then they kill the unwise man or woman that hired the hit and take the rest of the money in a rush. It's an old murder setup used for centuries. Blackmail takes too long. They are an easy in and out operation. The second was stealing from Domingo. I'll let you know if my boss has plans to do the snake dance."

"Is she seriously thinking that route?"

"Yes, she believes the dance will send a strong message."

"But they might run before she decides."

Max laughed, "Yes, that is her plan, but they won't get very far. Her darkness and reach are far superior and there are always the cops."

The Tracker thought about the money. "What a bunch of stupid screw-ups. They're already dead."

She followed the two people to the airport. She read the additional file on them. The woman's name was Maureen Burrows. They were a brother and sister team. The sister's papers showed a prison record for stealing drugs. The Tracker wondered if she was still using.

The Tracker watched the young woman closely. She wasn't very pretty and could pass for a man. There must be some screws loose in that head because no beauty shop ever crossed the woman's mind. The roommate's hair was ugly. Her money was hidden and spent on drugs when no one was looking.

"Yep, once hooked, the woman can't quit. Maureen, girl, you are high."

She watched the man. "Now there's a person in total control, bluffing the world in a high stakes card game. He will be dangerous company. He's the leader but of what and how much more is he going to steal? Those are our questions."

The Tracker woman knew the con artist game and was ready. She also was super good at poker. She would remain in disguise until the final scene. It would be a dance with another snake. She looked at her partner.

"Won't they be surprised to see another two-headed snake?"

Her man looked at his newly obtained gold snake ring. He liked it and hadn't taken the ring off since the Tracker gave it to him. He knew it was custom-made, high quality gold with diamonds, and was very expensive. Tracker woman wanted him to have a gift. She informed him that it was from a private kill he helped do in Miami. The man she took it from needed to go down.

She was ready to work this gig for Max and her boss. The Tracker woman evilly smiled. They exited the plane in Los Angeles, California, as did the Burrows couple. She asked the young man at the rental car counter for a vehicle. She overheard the other two people ask about fishing at Big Bear Lake. She didn't need paper maps. She had been to this area earlier in her career. She wondered what the two people were going to encounter in this area. This location made no sense to her. Perhaps the location was a hideaway to meet someone.

Tracker woman did pick up the local newspapers for cleaning fish later. She knew where the bait shop and boat rental facilities were on the lake. They picked up old clothes at a thrift store and a few jackets. There were some rusty plugs and old poles, too. All they needed was new fishing line and a fish knife.

20   Charity Sponsored Day

AFTER THE DISASTROUS Specialty Test Run Race, the police let the officials reopen the speedway. They didn't want to have a mass picket ensue from all the fans in town. The race car fans and their extended families bought their tickets and reserved their campground spots months ago, not to mention all the cases of beer stored in their RV's. They wanted to party, relax, and enjoy the show again.

Dan was recovering in the hospital for a few more days with extra security around him. The bullet went right through his hip area and did no major damage, but he would have to pass on this race and wait until the next one which was in Miami.

Tiare and Mic visited him with a case of root beer and a stuffed toy black panther. Everything was in clear cellophane in a nice basket. There was a package of new blue cotton underwear just like Mic had promised him on the track, only he bought extra, extra small. There also was a jar of tomatillo sauce and taco salsa included in the basket.

Tiare ordered Dan a fast-food delivery of cheeseburgers and fries for the next two days for lunch. Dan told them the hospital food was something they should donate to the old folk's retirement home across the street except the breakfast burritos were good. Hence, the reason for the jars of sauce.

Dan wanted to show Tiare where his wound was located, but Mic told him, "Nothing doing, I know you don't have any underwear on."

Tiare smiled, "Seeing his wound doesn't matter Mic. I've seen it all anyway."

They left a depressed Dan to try his wound game on the next woman to enter his room which was a real pretty nurse. Dan thought she would fit nicely into that new pair of men's underwear. He started feeling better already and was up walking around on his floor checking his surroundings. Dan gave a lot of patients and their visitors his autograph because it couldn't hurt to have a few more fans.

Dan was enjoying all the attention from the other drivers and their girlfriends that visited. The girlfriends brought their single friends in tow. Dan met a few new prospects besides the nurse and would get back in the game as soon as he could walk a little better.

The T-shirt shops printed some new ones that contained a picture of a drone with the words, "Test Run" imprinted upon them. The shirts sold out in the first hour. Tami bought two for Cortez and his brother to wear during the race. They should look like all the other normal crazed fans. Cortez wore the sling shot in his back pocket much to the consternation of Security.

Cortez thought, "You never know when some small thing would come in handy."

Cortez knew how to turn the sling shot into a snare. The brothers picked up some rope at the local hardware store just in case.

The police picked up the pieces of the drone to try to piece it together to find out the manufacturer. Of, course, it would be a company that recently went out of business and all records were missing plus the owner had died in a car accident recently.

The Charity Sponsored Race was a hit with everyone. Mic placed seventh because his game was a little off due to recent events. His black panther test car was also a wonderful hit because the company and race track decided to use the vehicle as a promotional tool. The sign read, here lies the only new race car to escape a drone. Congratulations to Mic Palla for his spectacular finish in the Specialty Test Run Race.

The car was placed in a special area. The fans could take pictures of themselves with the new race car. There were palm plants brought in and placed around the vehicle. A large stuffed black panther with a rhinestone studded leash collar sat on top of the black car under a gold velvet cape. There was a drawing box available to put a person's name and address for the chance to win the toy, a poster of the newly-designed car, and an 8x10 inch, hand-autographed picture of Mic Palla. The speedway officials included a life-size cardboard picture of Mic with his trophy in the display. The printers worked all night to finish the job. The cardboard picture was second prize. Third prize was a ball cap with the panther picture and Mic Palla. There was a sound recording of the race that played at the start of the hour. The line to the special exhibit was super long and busy all day. The exhibit increased the number of fans who switched their favorite driver at the race tracks over to be on Mic's side.

The person who hired the drone moved off the track. He needed to find the people he hired. They had to try again. The damage was not nearly enough. They owed him more for the money he paid. Their failure and his disapproval of that fact would fuel his fire. The drone hit man tried to visit Dan in the hospital, but there was too much security. The targets were Mic and Dan except they didn't understand. The police, however, were seeing the bigger part of the puzzle. Both race car drivers were in trouble from an unknown.

Derek and Rhonda still needed to talk with Mic and Dan. They thought if they brought the two of them together, it might jog their memory regarding Sawyer and Trent Rudy. It would be a good strategy.

21 Meeting with Mic and Dan

BOTH DRIVERS SAT quietly in the conference room. Dan moved his body in the chair. His wound was beginning to heal which was good. However, his leg was still stiff and sore. He hoped there was enough time for the wound to heal so he could drive in Miami. He knew that he was lucky and strong. He didn't bring his cane. He didn't want to use it in front of the other drivers. He got to the meeting early because his movement was still slow.

Derek and Rhonda came into the room with their coffee and sat down.

"Good morning, boys, we'll try to make this as short as possible because we know you both have busy schedules. I'm going to let Rhonda give you the information she has found."

Rhonda opened her folder of papers. "Here are photos of a dead man who we believe is Kevin Sawyer. He was beaten in the face and strangled. Do you recognize him, and have you seen him lately around the tracks?"

Both men looked at the picture. Mic said, "I don't think either one of us has seen him in seven years, right Dan?"

Dan shook his head. It was a long time. Years could change a man if he let himself go. It looked like Sawyer did exactly that.

"Plus, we don't really notice the fans too much when we are getting ready for a race. I don't recall the man anywhere around the tracks or concession stands. Dan, did you notice him around your pit boys or the garage area?"

Dan shook his head in agreement. He couldn't recall anyone at the tracks that remotely resembled Sawyer.

"Can you tell us a little bit about your encounter with the man when he was racing?"

"Well, we never liked him. He always cut corners and that's literally. He was rude to everyone. When he drove race cars a long time ago and was in the same races with us, we were green. Yet, we figured out the tracks and drivers real fast. Both of us have a head for speed and control. I think those facts surprised Sawyer. Then he was promoted somehow to the team manager. We weren't sure how that came about, except he was friends with Trent Rudy. Rudy also wasn't liked and was always in trouble with the officials. One time we caught Rudy smoking marijuana, but we never told anyone. Perhaps we should have," commented Mic.

Dan interjected, "The worst part is that we both saw Sawyer and Rudy talking to these unsavory guys who were arrested for fixing a race. We did testify to the racing commission those facts when they showed us pictures of the jailed men. I'm the one who convinced Mic to go to the officials. He didn't want to touch it, because he was the greener horn. But he was winning, and the race commission always talked to winners. We think Mic's information about what we had seen worked or at least helped to get both Sawyer and Rudy cut from the racing world permanently."

Dan stopped. Mic looked at him and frowned.

"Go on."

"Then Mic and I major disagreed about my dating his ex-wife Alexa. I took her to all the sponsorship dinners. It did take the commission a while to make their decision about Rudy and Sawyer, so Alexa and I ran into them a lot. I wasn't making that much money back then. Sawyer owned a bundle that he saved and talked of going to live in California. Sawyer waved his money around and played Mr. Hotshot. About three months later, she left me and went to California with the money-man. I think she was seeing him on the side. Sawyer convinced her there was more money on the table even if the commission dumped him. He didn't believe they would do it and we believe, that surprised him even more. Sawyer planned to stay in the game. The more money theory was probably trumped-up garbage to influence Alexa. However, we weren't sure about the guy, Sawyer, anymore."

Mic said, "We have recently seen Trent Rudy around the tracks earlier in the season, but not this past week. I even talked with him and there didn't seem to be any animosity. He told me that he converted cars, expensive ones, and brought them back to life. I figured that he was also doing fine monetarily."

Rhonda looked at Derek. "There's a huge connection. Both of our suspects were in California and Mic's ex-wife left with Sawyer."

Derek responded, "Yes. Both men's statements today show important links."

"Sawyer's dead body was found in a run-down seedy motel. The police believe his money ran out. He may possibly have obtained information on Rudy which caused Rudy to loan or give the man fifty thousand dollars which is missing. It is possible Sawyer ordered the hits for the tire bombs and the drone shot. We talked with Rudy about the money and received zero information. Rudy was also somehow connected to a woman in Miami. Now it seems Rudy is missing. We believe he has exited the area due to Sawyer's murder," commented Rhonda.

"Then there is your second wife, Mic." Rhonda looked directly into Mic's eyes.

Mic didn't know what Glamour had on him. Sometimes he ran into problems with women. Alexa was one of those women. But she was beautiful back then. Sawyer also noticed and liked young, pretty women.

"What about my second wife? How does Alexa come into this picture? I haven't seen her since forever. All she wanted from me was a million dollars which was a stretch back then to acquire, but I did it. As a man obsessed with anger at losing my wife, it was easy to pick races where I could win money and more sponsorships. The winning spree continued until the anger died down. I paid her off within a year."

"We have your financial information from the period when you knew Alexa. We also found out what happened after she spent your million bucks. She quickly married Sawyer in California."

The information made both Mic and Dan sit up. They hadn't known about the marriage.

"Sawyer's first wife had an accident on a scuba-diving trip back about the same time. Sawyer told the police he lost track of his wife briefly and surfaced to the scuba boat. He said he did that to get help once he figured out she was lost. When they found her, she was in sixteen feet of water. It was too late, and she was out of air. She drowned. Her line appeared to have gotten caught under a rock. Several rocks were moved on the ocean floor, but the police didn't hold Sawyer as a suspect. They couldn't prove how or why the rocks moved in the area. Sometimes a pile of rocks could fall when a large shark bumped into them or a large boat rudder hit. During this time, Sawyer already met Alexa and was secretly dating her. Without a wife to contest a divorce, he obtained the works, or should we say, bundle. He was flush with money to the tune of eight million. Alexa obtained half of his money in the divorce after only a year of living with him in California as a new second wife."

Rhonda checked on Mic. This next information might be a surprise to him or not.

"Alexa's married and divorced now about eight times. She has played and won the husband lottery very well. Her lawyer belongs to a prestigious firm who dug up major crap about Sawyer and his past women. Plus, she played the card about how he talked badly to her most of the time. There was a lot of dirt about his other wife's money and how he wouldn't let her buy nice things. It was the normal junk one hears in a divorce. Alexa used it eight times. The court records were almost a repeat in sentence structure about abuse. She must have memorized her pitch, or the sharp lawyer kept it as a word document."

Mic said, "Man, she used that same crap with my lawyer when she wanted my hard-earned winnings. She hasn't changed much. There is no true love in that broad. It's a wonder she's still alive and rich. Geez, I hate it that she is rich."

Rhonda and Derek smiled.

"She also has so much security surrounding her rich castle that we had to wait a while to get inside to talk with her. Alexa didn't like the guy, Sawyer, and is very glad that his body is on a cold slab at the morgue. She was delighted he couldn't harm her or ask her for his money back. Evidently, he has asked just recently for money. Alexa turned him down, and he was escorted off her property when he threatened her with bodily harm."

Derek interjected. "She didn't call the police but let things go. She told us Sawyer was more than a poor choice. He was a nightmare that she owed a small favor of nondisclosure. Now that Sawyer was dead, she gave us a copy of her security tape of the incident. The tape only shows the back of him and his voice confirms her statement about the threat."

Dan could see Mic's anger. "So, between our disclosure to race authorities, my introduction to Alexa upon Mic's divorce, and Alexa shaking every man down, we were considered the bad guys at the scene? Sawyer blamed us for his lost career and lack of money. You think it's Sawyer who was the director of the disasters. Now that he's dead, there should be no more problems."

Derek took over the rest of their meeting. "Thanks, Rhonda."

He turned to Mic and Dan. "We think there could still be a problem. We don't know if all the hits are complete because the two of you are still alive. We would like to continue with our investigation, and the police have agreed. We also need to find Mr. Rudy. Is there any place he liked to travel or visit frequently?"

"Fishing. The man liked to fish a lot. You give him bait and a small aluminum boat, it's his style. There was one place in California, but I can't recall the lake. I'm sorry. Dan, do you remember it?"

"Nope. I didn't listen much to his fishing stories." Dan was getting tired. He also felt good that he hadn't wasted too much time on Alexa. What a lethal woman she turned out to be? He looked at Mic who didn't seem happy right now.

Dan smiled and hoped it ruined his evening just a little bit. Dan dug out a piece of gum that was in his pocket and started blowing big bubbles. Mic hated it when Dan chewed gum.

Derek saw the taunts and rivalry between the two men. He could understand their endurance as overachievers in all the areas on and off the tracks. Derek saw Rhonda smile.

"We have a good friend named War Julio Samba and his lovely wife, Janet. They will be at the race in Miami as well as my wife, Jess. Rhonda's husband and many other Miami friends will be there. Janet's family have this huge fish restaurant on the waterfront. You may know of the place. The restaurant is Beach Buoy. They will close the restaurant for our party. We would like to extend an invitation to both of you and your guest on Monday evening at seven. We want to give the drivers a day to recuperate from the race. War Julio is providing the entire dinner and drinks, which will be massive quantities of exceptional fish and steak. I'll be paying for the security on and off the water plus the valet parking. Both of us own yachts which will be anchored off the restaurant. We've already been given approval. What do you think? Can we count you in our guest list? I warn both of you that there might be pictures taken and signing of autographs. Our crowd likes the racing circuit."

Mic perked up. He liked the Wright's friends and their yacht. Tiare would be with him at their lovely party.

"Absolutely."

Dan liked the fact that they included him. Mic's enthusiasm was a bright note in the room. Dan was curious about the change in attitude. "Yes, I like a party, and I've been to the restaurant. It's a great place, the best food, and nice ambience. There were lots of pretty women the last time I was at the place."

Derek and Rhonda stood up. "I'll let War Julio and Jess know. Good day both of you."

Rhonda walked past Mic and whispered, "I liked Tiare's bracelet. Very artful and perfect."

That made Mic forget forever about Alexa.

"Stay safe."

22   Big Bear Lake

TRENT PICKED OUT his live bait and drove back to the empty cabin. He put his thermos of coffee and sandwiches into a spot on the aluminum boat seat with his backpack. He threw the lifesaving cushion on the wooden seat along with rod and reel and fishing net. He felt for his fishing catch and release gear in his side pocket. He thought that he might keep a bass today if he caught one. Dinner and a good-sized bass sounded like mighty fine eating. There were canned potatoes and peas that would go well with the dinner. A little tartar sauce wouldn't hurt either. He picked up a few free packets at the Fish Hut.

He pulled his sunglasses from his shirt pocket and plopped his khaki-colored hat on. Shoving the aluminum boat out, he jumped into the bow of the boat. He checked the anchor rope to make sure it was tied correctly. Breathing in the fresh air, he was mighty glad to be away from the big city. Using the oars, he pulled on them to take the aluminum boat farther from shore before starting the motor. The water was shallow where he launched and there was no use in bending a prop. He groaned because he left his cell phone on the kitchen counter today at the cabin. He thought about going back for it. He liked to read the news on the darned thing. Perhaps he could fish some and leave early or he could watch the other boats on the water. The smell of engine fuel permeated the air as he pulled on the motor cord. The engine instantly came to life and he took the handle, steering his craft toward deep water.

A little way down the shore, another bigger speed boat went into the water and started their engine once they saw Trent moving. Every day, the man drove his tiny boat to the same spot. There was a large drop off where a school of fish came. The big fish waited every day for a smaller fish to cross the line. As the water warmed, this happened frequently. Trent saw the small fish jump, trying to get away. It was the way things were in a large lake. *Kill or be killed.*

The large speed boat with two people, a man and woman, would cruise the lake some and then drop anchor to watch the man. Their vigilance was tireless. Waiting didn't bother them at all. They were like the big fish in the lake. Time was on their side. The man in the aluminum boat was unaware.

A third small boat with an old canvas black top followed the two people in the larger boat and trolled the lake. The third small boat contained a woman with a high-powered rifle with scope. The gun was wrapped in an old gray wool blanket. The gray color matched the aluminum. The Tracker woman's super-lensed camera took pictures of the occupants in each boat whenever they appeared. The canvas cover was perfect to hide the lens. She poked out a round hole in the plastic window. No one could see the hole from her distance that she closely monitored. Careful to maintain her cover and distance, she on occasion put her net in the water in case anyone was looking. She uploaded the photos in the evening to her computer to review them. Her counterpart was left on shore sleeping in the rental cabin as he would be on watch in the evening.

The Tracker woman did her research. The man's name was Trent Rudy, a former race car driver who was now into reconstructing cars in his garage. The third evening, she unloaded her last grouping of pictures. There was a man on a fourth boat who met the second speed boat couple. The two boats were tethered together for over an hour. The man on the smaller boat looked vaguely familiar. "Of course, you are the former, cut-from-the-race circuit manager, Sawyer."

The Tracker searched on her computer and saw him on a race website. The man was younger and thinner. The hair was brown instead of gray. The old driver and manager in the photos had aged. There were creased wrinkles around the mouth and forehead. A belly flopped over the leather belt around Sawyer's blue jeans and white shirt. The shirt had a tire track design on it and holes in places. The man looked mean. The Tracker didn't care about mean. Mean could turn into a squashed bug at any moment.

The Tracker looked inside her dinner carton. She picked up the piece of meat and smeared the last of her dinner gravy while catching a pea pod. She crunched on the broken pea pod and swallowed the meat whole. Tossing the carton in the trash, she made a mental note to get rid of her garbage. She read another article on a newspaper website. The story was about an unsolved and recent murder.

"But you are supposed to be dead and are clearly not dust. Who was the victim? Do I care? The police were mistaken. What are you now up to with the Burrows? The Burrows brother and sister are in the speed boat, tailing Trent Rudy. The company around this lake is a strange group of people. Clearly, there are two teams of watchers. We are the third team in the game. This game is increasing. We are all watching and waiting for the same small fish to cross the line. Or are we?"

From the pictures, it looked like the Burrows' were arguing. They were pointing to the former race car driver in the small aluminum fishing boat. It looked like the woman told Sawyer to choose. She could almost read their lips. It was too bad they hadn't thought to bring a listening device.

Speaking to no one in particular, the Tracker said, "Choose what or whom?"

She put the newly-purchased and soiled chopsticks on her table. She didn't like the free and fat wooden ones, but these were better than spoons. Her partner sent her a message on her phone. The fishing guy left to go eat and the strange woman called Maureen entered the fishing guy's cabin and left. The fishing guy returned and went to bed.

Tracker decided she must go to bed. Tomorrow evening, she would send her report to Max. The Tracker woman washed the chopsticks and put them in her backpack. They were a tool she might need later.

XXXXXX

The next day Trent did the same thing that he did the day before. The lake started to get busy with the weekend crowd surging into the area. He hated to be on the lake then because there were always the big crazy boats. Trent picked up his plastic white flag with a large fish shape on it and placed the thing off the back, directly into the boat light slot so people would see him. He didn't drink his coffee because he put two cans of beer in his pocket. At three in the afternoon, he gave up when a speed boat almost ran over him. There was a man and woman in the boat. He cursed them, raised his finger in the air, and didn't think anything further about the couple until he reached his cabin.

Trent went to his cabin. In a half hour, he started quickly loading things into his car. He jumped into his vehicle and tore out of there before Maureen and Ed had tied their boat up. The Burrows' were delayed on the water before they could meet and pick up their friend, Sawyer. A water skier on another boat dropped off their ski tow rope and hit their speed boat. There was a deep cut on the swimmer. They thought about killing all the drunk students right there but knew there were too many boats who would see them. They weren't worried about Trent Rudy. He was boring to watch and did the same thing every day.

The Tracker started following the fishing guy, but saw the Burrows' were delayed so she stayed close to shore waiting for them to appear at the docks. She sat down on a small table with her computer. The Burrows' couple were the people she was wondering about. She, too, felt all right in letting Rudy return to his safe harbor, some friend's cabin, because the cabin wasn't listed as a rental. She found earlier the small sign kicked over in the grass that read, private.

The Burrows' figured out Rudy had left the area when they found his cabin door left wide open. They raced to their room and packed. Ed unlocked the trunk of the rental car and threw stuff in.

The Tracker woman followed with her computer which she stuffed into her backpack. Something was up. She called her man to pack, pick her up, and be ready in their vehicle. They noticed Mr. Rudy's car was missing from its slot.

Tracker had watched Maureen re-enter Rudy's cabin and race out of it. The Burrows' left the area at a high rate of speed. Tracker continued to follow them. There was only one road that would lead out of the campground area. The traffic through town would be brutal on the weekend. Tracker would drive the gravel right side of the road to catch them. Her partner would wear his costume and wave at the tourists honking their horns. No one would remember their vehicles.

Sawyer would know to leave when his friends didn't pick him up.

The maid would find the dead squirrel in Trent Rudy's cabin the next morning and call the police. There was a saucer of coffee and cream beside the poor thing along with some shelled peanuts. The police would think the squirrel looked strange and call one of their forensic friends. Normally, squirrels didn't matter except three cabins also emptied of their occupants besides this one which was supposed to be empty per the owner. Someone trespassed and fed the squirrel. The boats were at the dock except no one checked them back in or paid the remaining rental balance due. The rental people thought there was a scam of thieves who killed the wildlife. Obviously, the people weren't the fishing crowd. The fishing crowd at least paid the bill.

Derek would get a strange note from his Los Angeles forensics person and send his other investigator, Brandon Keller, to contact the owner of the cabin, the owners of the rental cabins, and talk to the neighbor tourists.

Sawyer ordered the Burrows' to kill Rudy. He wanted that hit to stand rather than a redo on the drivers. He didn't want to pay back the money owed to Rudy. Sawyer also saw Rudy's empty motel room. Sawyer knew how to drive fast cars and would run down Mic and Dan himself before the Miami race.

23   Pre-Race Ride Makes Friends

MIC SAT AT the restaurant in Miami and noticed Dan sitting alone at the other table with his bodyguard. Tiare wasn't due to arrive in Miami until two more days. Mic got up from his chair and went over to Dan's table.

"Well, aren't we a sorry looking mess? Two handsome, eligible, and let's not forget, popular race car drivers alone in a restaurant. We've shared women and seem to pick the same ones. Yet, here we are, all alone, once again. I hate sitting around without the women. I'm bored. You're bored. We truly are boring. No one even cares that we are here. Maybe we should try a different restaurant. If you are finished, why don't we dump these two ugly guys bodyguarding us and go for a cheap thrill ride? I have a super new sports car waiting outside which is a gift while I am here in Miami. The car dealership person told me that he was one of my biggest fans."

Dan looked at Mic. "We're boring? Isn't that a little harsh? There's no way that I'm boring."

Dan viewed the restaurant. The place was almost empty. It should have been full. He had no plans to give in to Mic Palla. "I'm just sitting here minding my own business, happy as a clam, I might add."

"Sure, you are. Let's hear the drum roll for Mr. Entertainer-of-the-year award. Whoops, he clams up when he reaches the podium. The man opens his mouth to speak and nothing comes out. He's either lost his mind or can't think straight."

Dan was used to Mic and his weird way of talking. "Mr. Entertainer. That has a nice ring to it. What kind of sports car?"

Mic knew he caught the man's interest. He pulled up the picture taken at the car dealership with two hot babes draped on his arm. The hot babes would get the racer off his chair.

Dan liked the expensive sports car, "Nice and a second nice. You know that I meant the car, right? Sure, let's do the free ride."

They drove on the freeway for a while away from the city of Miami when Dan noticed a car moving fast toward them.

"Hey, Mic, we have a fast tail that I'm thinking wants to play with us."

Mic looked at the car approaching which bumped his back end. "What kind of a stupid creep was that? Did you see the guy? It was a man. He looked big."

Mic stepped on the gas and the car turned into a rocket. Mic was flying off and on ramps that looked clear, not stopping at all. The tail was still riding his behind. He did a twirl through the dry center of the median to travel on the opposite side of the freeway. The car was still tailing him and came alongside.

Dan yelled, "Gun."

Mic swung into the car bumping it off to the side. The driver still tailed them on the right side. Mic stepped on the brake turning the car totally around and he drove the wrong way up the ramp on the opposite side of the overpass. He shoved the stick and flew down side streets traveling through the back alleys as if he was familiar with them.

Mic laughed. "I used to do this trip in my home town. The place was one of those small hick-towns where the only thing exciting was the train coming through at five o'clock in the morning. Can't you just hear the train whistle? I used to drive like this in my old man's pickup truck. I think it was robin's egg blue. They don't paint anything that color anymore. The birds hit the roof with white stuff every Sunday in the parking lot. They thought the truck was a nest with all the grass and hay stuck to the bottom rails. I drove that old blue pickup and flew the back alleys in my home town trying to get to church on a Sunday morning. My dad told me that I had to be there before the second song or my attendance didn't count. He wouldn't give me my allowance unless I made it to church. I was always late, so I had to pick up the pace. I cut it down to eight minutes from the normal twenty just, so I could get twenty-five cents."

"Your allowance was only twenty-five. Well, mine was a dollar and the coins were real silver. I guess things were better off with me. But I think that I would have liked to drive the blue pickup on the back roads with you. That spot seems like super-feel-good and totally untamed ground. The race to church episode is perfect fun; color me into the backroads. Maybe next time I can get lucky. You do know we are in a spot?"

They were somewhere out in the country with the crickets when Mic noticed there was no tail. That's when the road stopped, and they went soaring through an old wooden fence, landing finally in front of a huge and stinky pile of something. Dan's mind flashed black and white, and he thought he was going to die. Both men got out and looked at the pile. The sports car was up to its axle in something.

"What is this stuff? It's squishy," said Mic.

"Hey, small city boy, you can't tell the smell of shit?"

"Shit, no way. What kind is it?"

Dan scratched his head, "Well, it isn't from a cow."

"Well, Tex, then you tell me just what could be out here because I see two eyes coming our way."

Mic got in the car quickly and rolled down the window a crack. Dan dived inside the open car window because he was closer to the creature. Mic immediately rolled up the windows, fogging them up from the wet moisture.

"The eyes belong to an ugly wild boar. I saw it before the windows cloaked. We are so screwed," mentioned Dan.

The two men were silent while the boar grunted outside and ran around the red sports car. The car was a red cape in a bullfight.

"Tiare told you my nickname, darn it. She didn't tell you the story that went with the name, I hope?"

"Don't worry about it pretty *big* boy. She said something about stud-bull underwear and a lighter. They have strange stores in Texas where a person can buy anything. Except you need to read the label to see where that stuff is made. It could be hazardous to your health and super inflammatory. At least we lost the tail with the gun."

Dan was worrying about the inflammatory underwear. The tail on their vehicle was no longer holding any significance. The two men started to laugh.

"Shit," was the word both said at once.

"Where do you think we landed? We are located somewhere and need to call a tow?"

Mic went to the map function on his phone and waved the phone in the air. "The cell reads Astatula."

"Give me that thing, you typed it in. That city must be over two hundred miles away. We can't have driven that far."

Mic asked, "Well, why do you know how far Astatula is?"

Dan didn't want to tell him, but he was frustrated. He remembered the town because he ran out of gas there. "I got lost and my date was mad we missed a party. Let me tell you it was the most boring time of my life. It was worse than the restaurant we just left." He handed the cell phone back to Mic.

Mic called the tow people. "Hi, this is Mic Palla and I need a tow. We are some place called Boar a, Boar a."

Dan punched him in the arm. Mic gave the tow people the estimated directions and a description of the road. Mic and Dan sat in the pricey car and the boar wasn't going anywhere. The creature was looking at Dan's side of the car and suddenly charged, hitting the pricey door, and making a huge dent. Dan jumped toward Mic, almost landing in his lap.

"Oh, man, would you look at that door? That's unbelievable."

Mic was laughing and then stopped. The boar was moving to Mic's side of the car.

Dan looked at him as if he were in the car with some alien which was worse than the other pitiful creature outside. Then he worried about the alligators. He moved back to his side of the car looking annoyed. Fear and this mucky place were getting to him.

"Can a boar outrun an alligator?"

Mic looked out the window. He didn't see any alligators. He wondered which creature was more dangerous. The boar rubbed on the front of the vehicle, rocking the front end.

"How the heck do I know that fact?"

Then Mic thought he needed to lighten the mood and their situation.

"Don't you get it, Dan? Now we have more lift."

"What are you talking about? Man, your words make no sense. It was gibberish about clams in the restaurant and now this lift stuff," said Dan.

"The dent gives us more aerodynamic lift. The car will go faster once we get the glorious machine out of here. The boar did us a big favor and this car would work if we were on a race track."

Dan shook his head and watched the boar finally lay down under a tree.

"More lift, you are dreaming. First, they should attach a spoiler and lower this thing a little more. Then, yeah, maybe you could get more lift. By the way, I'm thinking that guy chasing us was a race car driver or possibly a former one. He reminded me of someone. I'll let you guess who," commented Dan.

"Yeah, those were my thoughts exactly. So, who hates us besides the exes?"

"That one is easy, Mic. I don't have ex-wives. You do. The who question is our mysterious guy tonight. He did drive exactly like our man that we didn't like at all in the good old days. It was Sawyer. You saw him try the same bump, and it was not clean. We've been behind him, in front of him, and beside him when he has cut us off at the race track."

Mic shook his head, "Like maybe he isn't dead after all."

"Yeah, I have arrived at the same conclusion."

"We're going to have to mention our thoughts to Derek and let him know Sawyer was always sneaky back then. We think he still is working the system to his illegal advantage. If he's alive, who was the dead guy?"

Dan sat there and looked at Mic. "Do we care about the dead guy? It could be anybody but count on it being some piece of dead space. That reminds me. You know what I hate about racing? It's the caution light and dead space. Dead space means us slowing down and waiting for the start of the race again."

"The wait doesn't bother me anymore. I have a new method that works," said Mic.

"What kind of method?"

Mic mouthed the words and when he saw Dan didn't get it, he clued him in. "*Think, boy, Hot Sex.*"

Dan sat there a minute and started laughing. Both men were cracking up. Dead space was the opposite of hot sex. Hot sex was space fulfilled. The caution light would no longer be a problem for Dan. He gave Mic a thumbs-up sign.

"We make a good pair," commented Dan.

An idea rolled past Mic.

Dan looked at Mic. "You know the fire truck boys at the tracks put more flame retardant on their trucks whenever we race."

"Is that right?"

"They have mentioned we are a hazard on the tracks. I overheard them say we are wheels of shit-fire waiting to ignite. They said it nicely."

Mic didn't believe Dan. "That is crazy. Maybe they said spitfire?"

"Nope, I heard correctly."

"Wow. Well, that's purely more purple bullshit. We just like to compete. You know, friendly competition, and we can do nice when we want."

Dan looked upward and liked the word, friendly and nice. "Where did you get purple?"

"Look out the window."

Dan rolled his window down a hair. The moon bathed the shiny slime.

"Speaking of the pig stuff, I hope our rescue team arrives soon."

Mic knew the timing was right. He was going to broach the subject with Dan. The idea was worth revealing.

"Maybe we should join each other and be on the same side. We could be wheels of spitfire, helping each other. The race track people would see a blur of purple stardust or moonlight flying past depending on the time of the day."

Dan hadn't seen the question coming. Mic was ahead of him again.

"Well, that idea threw me. More purple with good stuff thrown in. Where do you think up this stuff?"

"I don't know."

Dan blew out a breath. "This venture might work now that I'm dating the nurse, but we have contracts."

"There's always next season."

Dan nodded.

Mic thought about something. He remembered his conversation with Jim about lakes, alligators, and snakes. He wanted to rattle Dan to keep him off guard.

"Did you know alligators and snakes like these low cars, except I'm worried the dent moved the muffler just enough."

"Just enough? Mic, speak English."

Mic made a screeching sound to show Dan the muffler slide. "I've been told an alligator gets fried trying to eat a muffler off. Snakes, too."

Dan sat there. No response might turn Mic off.

So, Mic started making clinking noises with the keys on the stick shift and tapped on the dash. He looked over and wasn't getting any reaction from Dan. He pulled into the rhythm some noises with his mouth and rolled them out. It sounded like a rap song with a chain gang for a band.

Dan found some gum in his pocket which he started to chew. The gum chewing fueled Mic even more.

"That's the teeth working the already loose metal even looser. Too bad we don't have a case of beer."

Dan almost spit out his gum. He rolled his eyes. "You know you're one crazy person on and off the track. Did you even have a mama?"

"Yes, um." Mic started singing.

Dan knew he was stuck and screwed.

"My life was a challenge. Fortunately, I entered a state fair demolition-derby race. My mom encouraged me to enter. That's how I got my break. A real sponsor found me. The only problems were my sponsor owned a pickle factory. The car was a relish green color with a cucumber sign."

Dan was surprised. "You were a cuke-driver when you were young. I hear the train whistle in the blue-truck episode. Your whole life was filled with change. Well, that explains the hanging onto a rope and everything else. Wild and rut-roads is where you find space on the race track."

"Yes, that sums up my memories of untamed. I choose the track and space. We all know to avoid the dead stuff. What about you, Dan? Where do you travel, or do you select an open door?"

"I owe my entry to my parent's many friends. Sponsoring me was easy for them. I was an only child. Hence, the heavy emphasis on child-star. Then they found me a sponsor. The restaurant was well known for the ribs and bull riding machine. My first car was this ugly brown rawhide color. They put a pair of bull horns on my car. That was my open door."

"Horny and a slow door. Now I get the real picture."

There was no more judgment call by either of the men. Both race car drivers earned the right to be in the top circuit. Both encountered challenges. They no longer were greenhorns.

The men were silent. Mic would take a chance. Mic started humming. His voice mouthed the words to his make-up song. Dan listened.

"Two race car drivers lost in a country called Boar-a, Boar-a.
Brave it, trying to brave it. Boy, oh, boy.
Did we make a wrong turn, holding boredom away, away, away?
Oh, yeah, keep the beat boys.
Bop-a bop, bop-a bop, Bop, Bop, Bop.

143

At least we aren't the ones lying in the muck.
Brave it, holding the thunder. Boy, oh, Boy.
The villain, he did it, he's the one who got
away, away, away.
Oh, yeah, keep the beat boys.
Bop-a bop, bop-a bop, Bop, Bop, Bop.

Two race car drivers lost in a country called
Boar-a, Boar-a.
Brave it, trying to brave it. Boy, oh, Boy.
All we need is a big gun, then we can get out
of here, here, here.
Oh, yeah, keep the beat boys.
Bop-a bop, bop-a bop, Bop, Bop, Bop.

Let's get back to civilization, noise, lights, and
be in the clear.
Wait for it, trying to wait for it. Boy, oh, Boy.
All I can think of is women and beer, beer,
beer.
Of, yeah, keep the beat boys.
Boar-a, boar-a, boar-a, hairy boar-a, boar-a.
Ayah, Ayah, Ayah."

Mic kept tapping the rhythm and humming.

Dan's head started to move. He was feeling the
beat. "I'm kind of liking the sound. Now you're the
entertainer."

Dan joined in the sound after the first chorus,
tapping on the dash like Mic did.

"It's like the stuff outside. You get used to it.
I'm getting used to you. It's okay for us. We passed into
friendship. Am I seeing straight, is that thing snoring?"

Mic mentioned, "Same thing happened to the alligators and snakes, the falling asleep thing. I don't even hear the bugs anymore. We must be calming them down, too. The black and white vision that I saw earlier has disappeared. Yes, we are moving toward friendship and I'm glad. We are all right as race car drivers. We are competitors and then there is so much more to us. I'm glad you came on my ride."

Dan shook his head and wondered how they both saw the same scene earlier. He liked the song and was glad to be on Mic's side. The more he thought about it, they were similar in their attitude toward doing things the right and fair way. Dan nodded.

Mic saw the nod.

"I should get the rest of the group to join me in a crowd-funding venture. We could create a website of musicians that were current and former race car drivers. I bet there's a whole chorus and band among us. I know a few good buddies that might be able to join us. What do you think? Unless, of course, you can't sing."

Dan slapped his leg. "How did you know that I couldn't sing?"

Mic grinned. "Tex, maybe you could clean up after us when the gig's over."

There was no end to the male specimen sitting next to him and his off-the-wall babble. Dan wondered how to change the conversation. He lit up a cigarette. Dan rarely smoked but this was one of those required times. He was enjoying himself. He did, however, lock the doors earlier.

"No, seriously next year might work, being on the same side. You might look good in my colors. Oh, and you don't scare me."

"Your colors! What's wrong with mine?"

"You already got the girl. Now it's my turn," said Dan.

"Fair enough."

They repeated the song, singing out of sync with each other. The two men didn't care. A friendship was born. Mic grinned and then thought about the car dealership that owned the sports car. The dent would not set well nor the torqued underside, not to mention the mud or crap. The glorious machine looked like it was in a barroom brawl. Mic knew he probably lost a fan.

The tow truck finally arrived, having heard the singing and smelling cigarette smoke over the other cesspool smells. They had to call the Fish and Wild Game people to tranquilize the wild boar.

All the noise and lights from the tow truck brought out the farmer who owned the field. He brought his deer rifle and cell phone because the farmer had posted "no trespassing signs" everywhere. The farmer noticed the men didn't exactly see them. The signs were on the other road normal people drove. The boys missed the signs.

The racer boys let the farmer take a close-up picture of the two of them with the wild boar in the back of the large tow truck. Both race car drivers in the picture showed their hands on the rifle. They wore huge grins on their faces because they earlier stuffed an apple in the boar's mouth. There was an apple tree the boar guarded. The farmer loaded the picture to his computer and sent it to his friends. He wasn't very good at typing and wrote the caption on the note: Boor ah, Boor ah. The picture went viral.

The farmer invited the boys back anytime for a little homemade moonshine. He was glad they hadn't landed in his other field where he kept his bull. Then they would have been in much worse trouble. His bull wasn't afraid of boars or alligators. People were the bull's favorite toys. The farmer told them there was only one word they needed to remember if they were in a pickle with a bull in a field.

"What's that?" asked Dan.

"Run like hell!"

Mic and Dan invited the farmer to the Miami race and told him that he would have to leave his deer rifle and bull at home.

The farmer replied, "I'll be at your race. I'd like to see if you two boys know how to drive. From the looks of things, it's debatable."

The other race car drivers would hold hands over their mouths. The cameras didn't catch them. They made oink, oink sounds whenever they saw Mic and Dan together. Someone sent another team the farmer's website to view the picture of the wild thing. The only thing the drivers saw were three wild things in that picture. They all were mean and hairy looking.

24 Miami Announcers

THE MAIN ANNOUNCER was Tim and he loved the races along with the other announcer, Bill. The crowd specifically liked the show when they were listed on the race website. The Showmen were scheduled for the upcoming race. The various companies hired them as an entertainment team. The stands were always filled which was why the speedways worked hard to pull them into the contract. The two men kept their own fan club and knew how to manipulate the crowd.

"Well, ladies and gentlemen, welcome to beautiful Miami and the upcoming thrill for the day called the race. We are going to see lightning, well maybe slow lightning. How fast does lightning travel, Bill?"

"Just a second, let me look that one up. Have you seen my cell phone?"

"Maybe you have time to make a trip to the closest library. Naw, forget it, we'll look it up on our beer break. Oh, sorry, we can't have beer until after the race, not like all those crazy fans holding tight their beer thermos and smuggled roadies. They probably can't even walk the mile and a half oval track by the end of the race. No, seriously, folks, we have a great line up today of drivers, race cars, and terrific sponsors. The party was going to start. We've been told to get all our jokes in, because time's a wasting."

Bill came on, "Sorry, but you would need to add three more zeroes to our highest speed record to travel as fast as lightning."

"You mean like in the hundreds of thousands of miles per hour. Good lord, is that what they call grease lightning? You'd need a track made of asteroid turf before you could approach the banking turns. Besides, what would you call that kind of racing? It would have to be modified something or instead of open wheel, just call it freaking-flying-thunder wheel. How the heck would you brake at that speed and what about the caution flag? It wouldn't even be visible. The shape of all the speedways would have to be rebuilt so the drivers could find their pit areas easier. Bill, you boggle my mind. Where did you find that information, on some government website? You're not listening. I can tell. You've been paging out on me since 1995. You would think you were a driver in the 500-Series on an off-shore Australian track."

Bill looked sad.

"What's the matter now? Ok, so it's only been since last year, not 1995. Sometimes I like to stretch things for my audience."

"My grandpa had an old white horse struck by lightning. His name was Grease."

Tim shook his head, "Sorry is a good word for this dialogue. Let's pick up the pace, Bill. What gossip have you heard around the track lately? I saw your electric car the other day all over the areas where the driver's motorhomes were parked. You were having a nice day of it."

This is the part where all the drivers paid attention. They hoped the gossip wasn't about them.

"I heard there were two of our drivers who needed a tow."

"No, really? Was the tow required due to a bad tire or did they run out of gas? You can tell me. I promise not to tell anyone."

Mic and Dan stopped what they were doing on the track.

"There was a tow truck driver who told me the story. The two boys got stuck in Bora Bora. That's not in Florida anywhere that I could find," said Bill.

"Isn't that some tropical honeymoon place? You told me there was a juicy part to the story."

Bill laughed, "Yep, the boys were singing when they pulled up."

"You mean like serenading each other?" responded Tim.

"Yeah, and they were stuck in muck."

"Well, that's probably what's going to be spread on the track today with all this heat. The asphalt is going to be a sinkhole. This isn't one of the tracks with the concrete turns. Wouldn't that be nice? But the humidity should make things better."

"The moisture in the air makes the carburetor stick."

Tim frowned. "Are you kidding me? Is the moisture higher in Bora Bora because my wife is looking for a new sauna place?"

Mic and Dan breathed a sigh of relief. They were in the clear. The conversation moved off them. There wasn't too much damage to their reputations yet.

Tim said, "We've been given the sign to wrap up because we have to hand our microphone to the real announcer guy. You know his title is Commentator. That clarifies things to us a little better. We are like short-fry or stick. I do like the concept of first; how about you, Bill? We're like the racers at the front line ready to slaughter our opponents. Oops, I mean gently nail them where the sun doesn't rise. Did I say that correct? You should be careful nowadays. Everyone is policing slang words. Anything connected to the word, first, is high on their suspect list. But don't worry, the commentator guy invited us back for the last five laps. That's a good sign. Are you ready for hot dogs and cola? Bill, hello, Bill are you with me? Put that flask away."

Bill said, "My drink is lemonade for my cola."

"Yes, it is. Let's chow down cause the loop-de-loop show is about ready to begin. All those suits are in their shiny tattooed vehicles and the gasoline fumes have reached the tenth floor. The whine of the engines soothes my soul. Did you hear the rivet spin from the tire guys with their special guns? They can only carry three guns in the pit. That's a crying shame. The guns are monitored, too. What will they think of next?"

"I didn't know there were ten stories to this stadium? How can five guys handle three guns? Guess they have to share."

"No, some of those pit boys are changing the tires. I was checking to see if you were paying attention because you spilled some of that brown lemonade."

"The lemonade is brown from a little iced tea."

"Sure, it is, just like that muck. You know what they call bull muck in Texas? No, no, don't say it cause we're on the air. Well, are we getting the sign to shove off? Ride on, race boys. Hang tight to the front line. Talk to you later."

Tim turned off his microphone. Bill handed his to the commentator who just walked into the private top tower room. Tim's manager gave them each a high sign. The crowd was warmed up and cheering loudly.

25   Miami Race

MIC GAVE TIARE a kiss. He was called to enter the race track. He walked through to his awaiting team. Wearing his sponsor-tagged suit, he saw Dan sitting in his vehicle behind him. Dan mouthed to him, "Hot sex."

Mic gave him a thumbs-up sign and smiled. He placed his helmet on and entered his vehicle. They placed the pads down and ensured all the safety equipment was in place. He was ready and would wait until his car could move into final position near the starting line.

They were no longer antagonists but both racers who wanted to win. Each one would watch for the opportune moment to groove and move ahead. Mic usually was better and a step ahead. They placed closely in a race most of the time. This race was only three hundred laps which was good because there was more than the track heating up.

A cheap hit person had been hired. He approached the stadium and saw the stationery extra people that were possibly cops or someone working with them. He saw the extra cameras and there was an exceptionally long line through the gate. Security was checking identification as well. He palmed his badge and checked his uniform one last time. He should be able to get into the garage area with his badge. He kept the special-made bolts and nuts in his pocket that were sure to fail in this heat.

The hit person made it through main security into the speedway and walked toward the garage. There was a line checking the workers and their badges. There also was a metal detector. The hit man turned around and left the stadium. He wasn't going to wait for his extra man to appear nor the other man named Sawyer. The hit man knew he would be caught and didn't want to sit in some Miami prison. The police were all over this race track.

Sawyer was late getting to the tracks. He encountered several problems. First, he went to the local grocery store. He could smuggle the cheaper water into the stadium. There was a small store that he thought would be faster than the Quick Market two blocks further. All he needed was bottled water and maybe a donut.

He moved to position himself in the ten-items-or-less line, feeling confident that he would have time to catch the city bus to the stadium. There was a nice woman who seemed to have 18-20 items in her cart just a step ahead of him. The woman was obviously a cheater or couldn't count. The woman smiled at him.

"No problem. He was not in a hurry. No, sir, the nice lady could go ahead of him." He began to relax.

Then she pulled out forty coupons and hid them under her arm. She proceeded to ask for five bags of cat litter, five bags of water softener salt, a pile of wood, a carton of cigarettes, stamps, and ice. The clerk went to get a second cart.

"Oh, I forgot the beer."

The clerk went off to get the woman her beer. The other clerk rung up the extra items quickly.

Sawyer breathed a sigh of relief when the second clerk delivered the beer.

"The butcher is cutting me ten fresh pounds of ribeye steaks and bringing me more peppered bacon. Could you get those items for me?" She smiled at the second clerk. He nodded and disappeared.

After five minutes, the checkout clerk paged the meat department. The woman looked perturbed when she plunked down her purple-dyed snake leather purse on the counter. Her red long fingernails were tapping on the coupons she plunked down.

"Perhaps we can do the coupons now."

The checkout clerk saw the line of people behind his counter. The man next to the woman looked crabby even though he ate half his unpaid donut. The rest of the donut was crushed in the napkin. The checkout clerk knew he was in trouble when the woman grabbed candy bars and gum to add to her items.

Sawyer looked at the other lines in the store and they looked full. He couldn't move. The coupons were quickly rung up. He breathed a sigh of relief.

The woman wrote a check for part of the groceries and then put $7.75 in silver coins on the counter. The balance on the sales ticket read $7.78. The checkout clerk counted the coins. The woman was short three cents.

The woman responded, "Please recount it."

Sawyer quickly fished in his coin purse and threw out the three pennies.

"My treat today."

The woman thanked him. He nodded. His thoughts were that he wanted to strangle the woman. Sawyer saw the security camera and decided there were too many witnesses. He threw a five-dollar bill at the clerk for his water and donut.

"Keep the change," while he ran out of the store to the bus stop. There was no city bus in sight. He threw up his hands. He was out-maneuvered by a *nothing-else-to-do* woman in a short line at a market. He almost lost it until he saw a different bus approach. He waved his arms to flag the huge vehicle to stop for him.

Sawyer was on a bus on his way to the speedway. The side of the bus was printed special charter and the upper bus sign read Miami Speedway. Sawyer grinned and felt he was lucky. This one bus seemed to appear out of nowhere. He climbed aboard and gave them his money. The bus driver smirked.

Then the bus broke down five miles away on the freeway. Sawyer's thoughts made him wonder about his situation. Perhaps he should have stolen a car. Another bus was supposed to arrive to pick up the stranded passengers. They waited an hour and no second bus.

Most of the passengers got off the stranded bus and were picked up by their friends. The only people left on the bus were an old man and Sawyer. Sawyer kept glancing at his watch. The old man kept watching

Sawyer which made him feel creepy. He worried about this odd bus. Paranoia was rolling in. The bus driver told him the second bus would be delayed about another thirty minutes as there was a small accident on the freeway.

After another hour went by, the driver told the two men that the second bus wasn't coming. A third bus would pick them up in forty-five minutes. Another hour went by, and there was no one there to rescue the two men. Again, the driver told them it would take a little longer. The third bus was getting gas.

Sawyer gave up on this stupid bus scenario and started walking in the hopes he would see a taxi. He walked over a mile and a half when he saw the stranded bus fly by him with the old man inside. Sawyer waved to the driver. The bus driver didn't stop. The old man tipped his hat to Sawyer which pissed him off. No taxis stopped. Then there was a lone taxi with a woman driver who stopped. She dropped him off at the race track finally.

"Have a nice day," the woman driver commented.

"Thanks. I don't know where you came from, but you saved my life. It was important to get here."

"You owe me one." The taxi driver nodded and drove off.

Sawyer thought her comments were odd, but then his day so far was more than off. His instincts were warning him that something was screwy, but the clock was ticking. He became focused on his main objective which was to ruin a race for two drivers.

XXXXX

The race was in progress and the cars were reaching the last final laps. The drivers were positioned, not letting anyone pass to bump them down in line. The tension was building.

Jess and Derek, Jim and Mary Beth, Rhonda and Skid, War Julio and Janet, Tami and Cortez, and Tiare were in the enclosed VIP area enjoying the race. The rest of their families were in the stands also having a good time. Derek was glad everything had been calm. He thought for sure someone would try to infiltrate the garage. His teams helped the police check out any strange people. The garbage cans out front were constantly being emptied because they were full of things people shouldn't bring into the speedway.

Mic and Dan were racing well, staying close to each other, and weaving their way forward. They were in good positions which were six and seven, up one, from where they usually were in the other races that day. One of the drivers ahead took the turn and got a little too close to the wall. He wheel-popped into the wall causing others to scramble around him. Some of the others hadn't changed their tires and Mic and Dan had. This allowed a nice slot with more speed which Mic and Dan took advantage of. They moved ahead to the five and six positions.

The fourth position driver's part failed, and he headed toward the pit road. That would cost him a lap. This moved the two drivers to positions four and five.

Tiare and the entire room in the VIP lounge were jumping up and down with their excitement.

Tim and Bill joined the announcer because it was the last seven laps. The Commentator handed the microphone to Tim. He needed a break.

"Well, folks, what do we have here? I see the drivers are keeping a good rhythm. The smoking tires are adding to their rhythmic sound. Don't you just love that sound? I see the track hasn't been too difficult to pass today or perhaps some of the players have changed their style. It's called stealing space, folks. The good thing is that it's perfectly legal on those tracks. See, there's a message here. Find that lightning car and put him with Thunder, the jacked-up horse for a driver, and then the speedway gets winners."

The third car hit a bump in the track and a piece fell off his tire pulling him to the far right. Mic and Dan moved up before the caution light turned on. The crowd went wild as did the announcer.

"Whoo Hoo, the two boys are not only serenading each other, they are doing a dance," mentioned the announcer.

He hummed a little Hawaiian tune. "Isn't this a wonderful day for a fast car show? We are seeing extraordinary talent today. See those ten lead cars. I bet a few of them will win today. Which one? Who's betting? We all have our favorites. The tension is mounting. We are on the last lap folks. The white flag has been waved. Anything can happen."

Tim took a sip of beer that was handed to him by Bill.

"It's Sid Crayman, Mic Palla, and Dan Jaehn in the top three positions, ladies and gentlemen. Can they hold it? Or will they move again?"

The final lap is always the one the fans remember. People were standing, and it was getting crazy. Mass tension was building for everyone. The curtain would soon fall once they crossed the finish line. The cameras were refocusing there. Others hung back to catch the show.

Mic noticed Crayman, who was in the lead slowed a fraction, and he took his chance blowing around him. The minute Dan saw Mic's head turn, the white marker on the top of the helmet was what he had been watching on occasion. Something was up. Dan caught the car motion and followed Mic. The two men gunned their engines, flat out racing each other to the finish line, at least two car lengths ahead of the other car. They crossed the finish line.

Several other drivers blew past following Dan's move on Crayman. Crayman developed a temporary problem with a piece of eyelash under his right distance contact lens but did make the final ten.

An excited Tim announced, "Ladies and Gentlemen, a fancy two-step put Mic Palla in the lead with Dan Jaehn in second place and Merv Wilson in third place. The board will show the final ten drivers."

Tim, the announcer, took another sip of his beer because he could hardly talk. He waved Bill away. He knew Mic and Dan, and he wanted to congratulate them on their terrific wins today. Tim would wait until the new party. Derek earlier invited Tim and Bill to their party Sunday.

"That's what you call a powerhouse race. Congratulations Mic Palla!"

Mic finished going around the track, stopped at the finish line, and picked up his checkered flag. He did a dance around his car waving the flag as if it were some exotic Hawaiian ritual dance. He bowed, threw kisses to the women, and the crowd went crazy. Mic drove to Victory Lane to talk with the Commentator and thank everyone.

He saw Tiare waving and he finished with the Commentator. He ran to her and swung her around. Derek and Jim quickly escorted the two lovers into their awaiting black security vehicle. Dan also was escorted into a second black security vehicle. Their teams and friends followed, exiting the stadium on a special road for the drivers while the fireworks display kicked off.

Mic and Tiare were invited to stay on the Wright's yacht for the next two to three evenings. Dan was escorted to War Julio's motorboat where he was invited to stay. Their cars, motorhomes, and trailers would leave the stadium. The drivers would meet their teams in Phoenix.

The security teams would move with them because the little friendly squirrel in Big Bear Lake died from Mamba poison. The man at the cabin fit Trent Rudy's description and profile. The police felt Trent was the intended victim. The police wanted to catch the criminals once and for all as did Derek and his team.

They knew things were royally heating up. They worried about Phoenix.

26   Beach Party and Afterward

THE MIAMI DELEGATES and officials arrived with their wives and massive security detail early to the restaurant party. They wanted to talk with the sponsors and enjoy the good food before the place was a mob scene. They knew Jess and Janet were going to put on a spectacular party.

Jess brought into town this special band from Los Angeles called, Terelle Triumphs. The music would be everything and anything. Terrance and Michelle Reston brought their friend who could play the Tahitian mandolin. Jess promised the show would be an exciting evening with the top two race car drivers present. Mic agreed to do one number. The delegates' wives were anxious to meet both drivers and hear the music.

Jess wore a new designer dress with a champagne and ruffle layer design which tiered around her. She wore her emerald and diamond necklace with the diadem in her upswept hair. Derek was in a white jacket tuxedo with black pants. He wore a champagne colored tie that she had designed. He hugged Jess.

"Thank you for the tie. It is so very you in style and color. This is going to be a fun party, honey."

"You are ready?"

"Absolutely, always, anything for my very beautiful wife. The special case of scotch has arrived. It should be a party."

"I have another romantic surprise for Tiare because Mic has promised to sing his love song to her."

"How did you manage that?" asked Derek.

"The arrangement was easy. He loves her."

Derek shook his head. He knew the wives in his group were planning something with his wife leading them. Jess was very good with people. She had won over the man's heart who loved Tiare. He was not surprised at all. Jess on a mission was a formidable foe. Derek laughed. He was confident that Tiare was in the lead as well.

"Yes, I saw all the food on the list. They even included their famous two soups, Clam Chowder and Grouper." Jess smiled. She saw her husband recognize her planning skills. Jess continued.

"War Julio insisted people would want the two soups. They have small cups. Our guests can just sip them down like an appetizer. Our chefs are trading recipes. War Julio has brought people from his other restaurants and the Cortez family has contributed as well. There won't be any food not scrutinized, tasted, and served at the proper temperature in this restaurant."

"Great, I can hardly wait to hit the fried fish section. I love it that our chefs are sharing their best. I heard War Julio mention something about the California Burrito with avocado and French fries. Tonight, is my splurge night. I'm going to ignore calories. You can eat all the vegetarian stuff. I see there are several pasta sauces on the list and delicious homemade noodles. Are the spoons metal?"

Derek looked at his wife. He wanted to remind her of other fun times.

Jess remembered. "Yes, my knight, we have real dishes and silverware. There is no plastic, fake, pretend anything here. The homemade pastas and noodles were on my list of things our chef should learn. The Miami food has different spices from our California world. I wanted to capture those tastes for our guests. We need to play both tastes at our other future parties along with the Curacao menus."

Derek kissed her one more time before he reluctantly let her go. They opened the door to their guests along with War Julio and Janet. Derek held his wife's hand. He was proud of Jess. She looked like the wonderful girl he knew on a Napa date night long ago. He could hardly wait for their guests to exit. But first, he must do this party. She was excited about tonight. Everything was to entertain and introduce the race car drivers to their group.

He looked out to see their yacht and War Julio's motorboat had made it to the Miami location. Jess arranged their schedules from past cruises. It was close getting both ships into the Miami bay with all the required permits. Both ships were anchored and lit with strings of white lights. Even the helicopter areas had focused red lights which shone. The scene was enough to scare anyone, or those in the criminal world away from their area. Their gun carriers on the helicopters were visible.

The police helicopters were on reserve if they needed them due to the high officials attending the party. Derek saw the fireworks barge in the distance. He thought Dean Crain, their old friend, would be proud. Derek did learn how to protect Jess.

Derek felt better having his wife and children with him. The children were so part of their world. Jess was his major focus. Whenever she was ready, he was ready. Their children moved to a combined team flow. That didn't count all their other close friends moving with them.

The dignitaries arrived as did Mic, Tiare, Dan, and the announcers from the race. Mic kissed Tiare and went over to talk with his friend in the band to do the set for their arrangement. Mic told Tiare about the request from Mrs. Wright. Tiare was pleased that Jess included Mic in the party. It sent a signal to her that Mic was accepted.

Tim and Bill intercepted Mic.

"Did you see the mayor is here and so many others?"

Mic replied, "No, I didn't, but why don't you introduce yourselves. I'm sure they would like to meet the great Showmen at the race who knew us two boys would win. I believe you already figured out the race as did we."

"You knew?"

"No, we didn't know but we're just better in the game."

"Great, that's my byline words into the dignitary world. Thank you, Mic. Good luck on your song. Jess told me that you are singing tonight. I would like to hear that. And, again, congratulations from us on your race win."

"Thanks a bunch," said Mic.

Mic saw Dan trying the soup at one of the elegant buffets on each side of the restaurant. He saw a young, beautiful woman approach Dan and knew he would be all right. Dan was smiling, lost in the young woman's conversation. Mic smiled because the woman was Janet's sweet and exceptionally pretty, favorite niece. Tiare showed him pictures of her important relatives so he wouldn't feel lost at the party. "Way to go Dan, pick the best."

Mic smiled. "This setup was going to be another amazing party." Mic saw the seafood buffet. He saw War Julio checking it out and talking to the chef. Mic would introduce himself shortly to the man who owned this magnificent restaurant. He waved at Jess and did a little dance. Jess pointed and waved her hand and body like a hula girl. He gave her a copy of his first tape of the song for Tiare.

Mic bowed. "Oh, yeah, definitely fun. Lucky Derek and lucky me."

𝒳𝒳𝒳𝒳𝒳𝒳

Derek and Jess stayed two weeks in Miami with their friends for a much-needed vacation. Derek felt rested and ready to tackle the bad guys. Jess gave him some insight into the killer's mind. She believed there were four sets of killers: Sawyer, Snake woman and her possible crew, the copycat snake people, and the politician.

"Why the politician? Do you believe the politician killed his wife? He more than likely hired the copycat killers to do the job. I don't think he would personally kill her. Murder in broad daylight would be too risky."

"He might have hired them, but I believe he became impatient and did the deed. I've heard through the female grapevine that she intended to divorce him. He would have to pay her a lot of money which may be part of the motive. I believe the real one was revenge. He couldn't have her walk away without some hurt. He wanted to hurt her, and he did just that. I think he was a person who wore a wig and a fake tattoo on his neck like the copycats because he does know who they are. When she called her husband, she realized he was standing in front of her. He was dressed like the fake snake people. He forgot his phone which was ringing. He saw her recognition right before he shot her. Then he used his phone as cover when the police came to his home. It was a perfect murder except for the tattoo. The photo the police took of him at his home showed him wearing a navy-blue turtleneck. The weather was ninety degrees that day, much too hot for those types of shirts. He didn't have time to wash off the dye or any debris. He covered the tattoo up. He knew the police wouldn't think to search him."

"The problem that I have is that your story is only intuition and conjecture. If we bring the politician into the police station, he will just walk out free again."

"Perhaps you can get a search warrant and find the wig, gun, or clothes and shoes. There should be her blood splattered on them because he was so close when he took the shot."

"He more than likely has thrown that away, along with any other evidence. We'll have to wait for further information. It would be nice if we could see the copycat's computers. I'm sure there are documents there that would incriminate him. If the copycats were smart, they would turn things around and blackmail him. This might be a good idea to see if we can capture the politician's financials. But, he has his highly successful team of Miami family lawyers blocking all my attempts. We are at a stalemate until something else breaks."

"Yes, I hope they catch him soon, because the politician has a new girlfriend. Their picture was in the newspaper next to a prestigious jewelry store in the Diamond Exchange building. I don't want him messing with another woman's life."

27   Tracker Watching

SHE FOLLOWED MAUREEN and Ed Burrows who pulled over to the edge of the road near a large, immaculately groomed estate with mansion house and high wrought iron and brick fencing. Tracker drove past and wrote down the address which was in gold letters on the lion heads over the wrought iron gates on each side. The mansion was set back away from the gate and was bordered by exotic plants.

Tracker pulled off the side of the steep roadway in a break between the houses. She could see the ocean. She pretended to take pictures of the view. Then she took one of the mansion. She got back into her rental car. She shot pictures of the Burrows standing outside their vehicle. Then she looked up the address on her computer in the county tax database to retrieve information as to the owners. The owners of the mansion were Alexa and Connor Griffith. They purchased the home nine months earlier for fifteen and a half million.

"This girl is definitely living fine in her world. You've got to hand it to her. She likes classy. But why are they watching her?"

Her partner was at their hotel room. Tracker pulled up Alexa's history and saw a name.

"Sawyer. The woman had been married to Sawyer in the past. Now I get the connection."

She dialed on her cell phone for Max.

Max said, "Let's see what they do. We need to know if they are going to shake this woman down or not."

"Isn't that a little bit drastic? Waiting might give the Burrows enough money to permanently disappear. You must convince her to change. I've mentioned this before. We could be too late for the dance."

She heard Max talking to Snake woman. She thought she heard a baby crying. That can't be what she heard. It must have come from her radio. She turned the car engine off but heard no further crying.

"The plan is always her decision."

"Yes, it is," reluctantly said the Tracker.

The mansion gates swung wide open. A silver limousine with driver and a woman in the back drove down the road. The Burrows hurried into their vehicle. Tracker started her engine. They drove toward the city taking the exit ramp into the downtown area. The limousine dropped the woman off at an exclusive beauty shop. Tracker woman annotated the name, address, day, and time.

The Burrows parked down the street and Maureen got out. She looked directly at Tracker who pulled into the parking slot. Tracker called her friend who drove to the area. She saw him and signaled to pull out. Her friend pulled into her slot and Tracker drove down the street and went around the corner out of sight.

Tracker knew they would need to change rental cars again. Maureen was acting too suspicious. Tracker looked at her pictures she took of Alexa entering the shop. Her partner texted that Maureen followed the woman into the shop.

"They are doing their own snake dance," said Tracker to no one.

Maureen's hair was trimmed, and she waited. The pretty rich woman was having her hair root color touched up. The beauty operator brought Alexa a small bottle of water as she pulled the bonnet hair dryer down over the woman in the plastic hairnet. She told her if it got too warm, she should just lift, and the dryer would turn off. Maureen slid into the next hairdryer and the beauty operator turned her dryer on the low setting to blow dry the wet hair.

Alexa opened her bottle, took a drink and left the open bottle sit on the small table between the hairdryers. She picked the ladies fashion magazine off the table and ignored the unattractive woman sitting next to her. She wondered how the woman could afford the prices in this place from the looks of her rubber shoes.

Maureen was a true con artist and jumped at the opportunity presented to her. She finished the hired hit. The man that ordered the hit was upset with them that they were taking too long. He wanted the kill done as soon as possible. They thought they better comply for now. They didn't want him to talk. This kill was to keep him quiet; his time would be up soon enough.

Maureen placed the small snake skin on the table next to the water bottle and walked out of the shop. She handed cash to the beauty operator and told her to keep the ten-dollar tip.

The Tracker drove around the corner and parked. She went into the coffee shop and bought coffee and an egg salad sandwich with lettuce. She ate half a sandwich and drank some coffee. Her partner texted, "They are moving."

She started eating the rest of her sandwich. She heard sirens approaching in the distance. Tracker slowly drank her coffee and finished her sandwich. She knew the fire truck and ambulance would be here shortly. The beauty shop would be cordoned off. The Tracker felt confident they found their copycat snake people and caught them in the act. There were only the two of them. It wouldn't be difficult to stop their next move. She felt Sawyer was only a client.

She contacted Max.

"When you find a good location for the two people, leave some information for the police. That is after you have entertained them and done a dance. Be sure to pull all files."

"We will take care of everything."

Derek was notified by the police. Rhonda met him after his flight from Miami and drove to their investigative offices in Los Angeles to talk with Brandon Keller. They were not surprised by the name of the dead woman. The name showed as Alexa Griffith. Someone finally did her in for her misdeeds. They believed Sawyer hired the hit. A vengeful, raging past husband ended the husband shopping spree. The copycat killers that Sawyer probably hired used the correct amount of poison this time. It took less than thirty minutes. Derek pushed the police to put greater emphasis on finding the real Sawyer and Rudy. Derek knew Sawyer was the killer. Rudy was in as much trouble as was Dan and Mic. There was an evil one on the loose. Either Dan, Mic, or Trent Rudy could be next.

Mic and Dan would feel bad about Alexa's death because they both loved her once. They would attend her funeral under heavy guard. Sawyer wasn't anywhere near the place. He would be setting up another meeting with the Burrows.

Sawyer would need to skip the Phoenix Race but would wait until the one in Fontana, California. Sawyer was going to lie low. The only thing was he didn't know how low he was going to have to hide. He might as well have turned into a street bum like Trent Rudy did in Santa Monica to escape detection.

28 The Kill

TRACKER'S MAN FRIEND contacted her with his location. She couldn't believe it. These two people drove to Big Bear Lake in California and rented the same cabin with the same speed boat. She didn't know if they were arrogant and brave or plain stupid. Maybe they figured everyone else was stupid. That had to be their mindset.

The Tracker was there to set things straight with them. It would be fun to watch their faces when they figured out who she was. The Burrows saw her in the small boat last time, and when she was going in and out of her cabin. They saw her in the small store, too. She let the Burrows' sister and brother see her without any disguise. The tracker was confident in her next move. These people were simply dead before she ran into them. They just didn't know it. A disguise was not required when she was around them. Every other place, she wore disguises. No one would remember her or her friend. The Tracker could hardly wait but must take her next steps carefully. Precision was key.

"This kill needed to be performed with no hitch. I'll pick up groceries for us first," she informed her partner.

Tracker arrived in the evening, because she watched the body taken out of the beauty shop and talked to some of the shop owners after the police left. The dead person was some rich woman in California that died.

The Tracker also switched rental cars there. She relieved her partner in Big Bear Lake, looking through the telescope at the brother and sister cabin. There was no movement. Settling in the chair, she opened her notebook computer and read the notes he sent her. He had written that the couple took all their bags into their cabin.

"Good, they plan on staying a while which would work to our advantage."

She called the Boat Rental place and reserved a large speedboat with a huge powered engine. Tracker gave them a new credit card, good for a five-thousand-dollar limit under a different name. She decided a disguise was required after all to lure the Burrows. Maureen looked suspicious again. Tracker took the hair dye out of her shopping bag and started squeezing the gooey gray color onto her hair. She retrieved the cheap glasses and set the can of chewing tobacco out along with a bright red handkerchief for her partner. She put the flannel plaid shirt on with her blue jeans and black tennis shoes. Soon, they would look like the local tourists on a vacation. They would blend into the crowd and become nobody. The new fishing gear was in the trunk of the rental car.

Tracker placed the case of beer along with the two syringes and vials in the refrigerator. She made sure the beer was the brand the Burrows drank. She put the cold groceries away. She put the potatoes, onions, and butter on the counter along with the box of foil.

There were several bags of salad and dressing with ten pounds of hamburger, just in case there was no fish. She eyed the salad dressing again and the small paper cups she would put them in. She didn't need different colored cups, because she knew Maureen and Ed always chose Ranch dressing. Ranch dressing would work because it had flavor and was a common item.

The whole American palate was based on ranch flavoring in chips, dressing, vegetable crème cheese dip, etc. The poison would work there. She needed to make sure the salads were eaten first. The potatoes and fish or burgers would come later, like about fifteen minutes would work if she had to add the obnoxious, poisonous drops. She looked at the frypan sitting in the oven rack. The heavy item was cast iron. The Tracker liked the dark metal in a kitchen. The pan worked as a debilitating weapon, if required. Things were looking good for an old-fashioned fish fry. Too bad they couldn't cook on the beach. The cast iron would have worked great over coals. The beach was not good cover. There could be a stray tourist arriving untimely into the dinner plans. Maybe some other time for that one?

She turned on the old radio and found a country station. The song seemed to be the only one that worked around this area. She kept the music low and rechecked the night scope. There was nothing moving.

The next day the Burrows walked with their gear down to the docks and got into their speed boat.

Every day, they dropped anchor in the same place. It was the drop off area that Rudy liked. Tracker and her man steered their speedboat to the same area and dropped anchor. The two couples waved to each other. At the end of the day, they went back to the dock and chatted a little about the weather, and where they were from. Each group made up their name and bogus homey stories.

The two groups did this same routine for two days. On the third day, Tracker used this special bait that the Bait Store kid told her worked to catch big fish. She tipped him every day to put her bait in the car because her friend was tired. She fibbed that her friend could barely climb into their rental boat. Her friend could lift the boat out of the water with no help from her and get it settled on the trailer. Her friend was a work horse. She waited until the last hour to use the bait. She readied her net and slinky hook line. This was going to be a great catch. She saw the large fish swim through the clear water the other day. The fish were checking her line.

Tracker woman landed a huge bass fish which flopped in the boat until she stepped on it to remove the hook. The other couple cheered. Tracker waved. Both boats left the area at the same time and reached the dock. Tracker invited them to a foil-potato and fish fry dinner with salad. Maureen was a terrible cook, so they agreed to meet at seven that evening. Food of any kind was better than the sister's abysmal attempts. The brother was hungry.

Easy kills were best. The brother and sister came to Tracker's cabin enjoying a round of drinks and conversation. The Tracker and her friend finished their dinner and threw out the other couple's meals. They were in one of the cabins that had a garbage disposal. Garbage disposals destroyed evidence. After midnight, they hauled the bodies out to the trunk of the Burrows' vehicle. They wrapped them with the thermal blankets from their rental car. The brother and sister were dead.

Using their keys, the Tracker and her friend entered the other couple's cabin. They searched through everything and then put the items back in the couple's large duffel bags. They took their computers and replaced them with new ones and sent each other a few normal emails as if they were the two people still alive. The new computers were bogus and contained nothing for the police. The Tracker and her man took the victim's cell phones and copied the data over into separate files to review later. The victim's cell phones were thrown into the lake. Tracker put a folder on the table with photographs of Maureen entering the beauty shop, Alexa's swanky house, limousine, and other photos for the police.

She reset the table in the Burrows' cabin with half-drunk open beer bottles, chips, and chocolate chip cookies. She put their groceries in the Burrows' cabin. The groceries would look like they planned to stay awhile. The hamburger or what was left of it was put in the freezer in patties in foil.

Tracker and her friend threw their own cabin garbage away, returned the speedboat, and deposited their fishing gear in the huge dumpster. They left the couple's keys on the kitchen table of their cabin along with their wallets. Setting the scene to look normal for the Burrows' couple was the goal. They didn't take anything out of the cabin, other than to check their fake id's. Their real ids were in their duffel bags. The real identification cards were thrown in the lake.

Tracker let Max know the outcome of the dance. Again, she thought she heard a baby in the background. Later she would have to fly to Russia, but not yet. She saw a name on the dead people's computer. The Tracker debated about telling Max of the name. It was hard for her to turn information over to her boss. The name could matter.

She would wait for a new assignment from her leaders.

XXXXXX

Sawyer arrived a few days later. He broke into the Burrows' cabin when there was no answer because it was raining, and he didn't want to sit in his car anymore. He parked his car some ways from their cabin in the visitor lot and needed to watch the cabin. He waited a day and then made the mistake of eating a fish burger at a restaurant nearby. The police would show the hostess a picture of Sawyer later.

Sawyer came back and opened the brother and sister computers. There were very little files which didn't seem unusual to him. The couple was secretive. He gave up and went to bed. It was better than sleeping in his rental car. The next morning the rain stopped, and the sun came out, heating up the trunks of the vehicles. He saw the photos in the envelope and didn't think that was unusual either. He cooked himself some eggs and toast, wondering why there was no sausage. He found the hamburgers in the freezer and thought about eating them later. He didn't know whether Maureen or Ed cooked. Maybe they only cooked the easy stuff.

It was getting late in the afternoon when he decided to check out the campground. Walking by the Burrows' rental car, he stopped. Something smelled bad. He suddenly recognized the smell. He hurried into the cabin after looking around. No one had seen him. He grabbed his gear and saw the wallets. He pulled out the money. Next, he checked the duffel bags and pulled out ten thousand dollars. He opened the manila folder and took out the picture of a partial view of him in the boat with Maureen and Ed.

"Who had taken the pictures?" He thought it was Maureen, but it couldn't have been her. Sawyer didn't care anymore. Something was off with this cabin and their disappearance. There was sufficient money for him to move on. He was going to leave the rest of the smell and lack of bodies for the police. He hoped Maureen and Ed would show up on the police's radar screen as the killers of Alexa. He left a piece of Alexa's stationery with their papers. Sawyer smiled.

Sawyer drove down the road heading out of Big Bear country. He felt confident he removed his prints in the cabin. A thought suddenly occurred to him, "They saw my face. That is not good. But they are dead.

Did anyone else see me there? The killers, they must have saw me. But who are they?" There was no doubt in his mind that the Burrows were dead.

Sawyer would lay low, out of sight. He could do exactly that thing with the new money. He would need to skip the Phoenix race and would wait until Fontana, California. The delay would give him time to work on his final plan. He knew some older, cheap motels around Santa Monica. He could go fishing off the piers and buy some gin. He really needed a drink after this fiasco. The killers worried him. The deaths started gnawing at his psyche. Sawyer knew he could buy cheap clothes at the Santa Monica tourist stores. He hoped they sold sunglasses because he left his on the counter of the cabin. They were nice ones. Would the police notice or get his DNA? He had been stupid. But the Burrows were stupider.

"Too late to drive back there."

He knew it was more than too late for his newly-found friends. They told him they were blackmailing someone. They said the man was a high-profile person in LA. No names were dropped. He wished the Burrows told him who that high-profile person was. He could use a little money-action game called blackmail.

Sawyer only remembered something that Maureen let slip. She called him rich playboy and a politician. The man killed his wife in Los Angeles. He would need to check the library for any newspaper articles. Sawyer hadn't followed the LA news scene. There had been no reason. Now, there was. His luck might be returning. Sawyer knew he was good at research. Research was only an extra little step and he could use more time before he killed.

The scale was beginning to tilt toward evil. Another con artist game would enhance the odds and become something much larger.

29   Derek at Big Bear Lake

DEREK WAS GOING to participate in the detail team to guard Mic and Dan at Alexa's funeral when he was called away to the murder scene at Big Bear Lake. He asked Brandon Keller to stay with Rhonda on the team and fill in for him so that he could take Jim Michaels with him to the death scene. Jim was very familiar with the area and would be a big help talking to the local people who knew and trusted him. They might reveal more information.

They approached the cabin and parked where the police told them. They saw the trunk lid open and went there first. Jim couldn't believe the smell.

"The pictures are all complete and the coroner will take the bodies in their bags. Don't touch anything, because we believe it's the same poison as the squirrel," mentioned the local sheriff.

"All right, here's the name of my Los Angeles coroner whom your coroner may want to compare notes. The call should make his job proceed more quickly. Can we check the cabin and contents now?" Derek handed the sheriff his friend's business card.

"Thanks, the information is appreciated. You can proceed to the cabin."

Derek and Jim looked around.

"I don't think they were killed here. Does this kitchen look a little like a stage scene to you, except the cast iron fry pan in the sink with egg shells and beer bottles in the garbage? Note, all the bottle caps in the sink don't match the number of beer bottles. We are two caps short like the two bottles on the table. I also don't think beer, chips, and cookies go with eggs," mentioned Jim. "The place looks like two or three sets of people lived here," said Jim.

Derek shrugged.

Jim pulled open the refrigerator and then the freezer. "Is this odd to you? Who makes hamburger patties and puts them in foil? Looks like a very precise, neat person. Those two don't look neat or like people that cooked. There's no foil box in the cupboards anywhere. Where did they get the foil? Besides, when I go fishing, the hamburger is left in a huge pile in the refrigerator. I don't stop to buy expensive foil. I just use the cheap cellophane from the store. There's nothing in the drawers to preserve anything. They didn't even use the dishes and there's no paper plates in their garbage. I think the hamburger and this whole cabin are a set."

Derek and Jim checked the bedroom and duffel bags which were empty. The clothes were thrown on the floor.

"Now this is more like it. Looks like there was an envelope of money in the small ruck sack as there's a bank envelope, but no money. Is the bank envelope real or is that a ploy? We'll need to check that one out," said Derek.

They went to the computers on the table. Derek wore his plastic gloves and lifted the lid, turning the computer on. "Nothing in here. There's no other files. The computers may also be a set. Let's look at the envelope of photos. I don't know if they are real or not. The picture looks like Alexa's house. The piece of stationery shows her name. This cabin set is unreal. It's like two people worked the stage. I think more than one person wanted to point us to look at the Burrows as Alexa's killer. I find this interesting that the killers would want to help the police."

"I agree with that assessment. Do you think Snake woman participated in this scene?"

"It's her signature possibly on the poison. I'm not sure. These deaths are not her style. The Burrows are small cheese. They were running and trying to gain ground. I don't think they made it in her world. I could be wrong. The Burrows could be connected to the Miami dead woman and Matin Domingo. Then, this kill would make sense. We need to ask the owner of the cabins who else was here the same timeframe and check out the boat rentals and bait shops. Also, possibly the restaurants. Those two-dead people seemed like the restaurant type. There's no ketchup, mustard, or relish anywhere in the place."

"Yeah, who eats hamburgers without ketchup, mustard, relish, and buns. Plus, there's no cooked fish smell in here nor any candles to chase the smell away. If the fish was the cause, the food is not here."

Derek shook his head. The two people in the car didn't know what hit them. The man was Matin

Domingo's ex-lawyer who probably robbed Matin of his account money. The sister was more than likely the dead Miami girl's roommate. He had seen part of the woman's rope tattoo.

"I think we have found the swindlers and copycats, Jim."

"Yeah, this murder scene looks right on. Let's check the restaurants first. I have a favorite that makes really good fish sandwiches."

They went to the fish restaurant and talked with the hostess. They showed her the two dead people's pictures. She recognized them from an earlier time they were there. She hadn't seen them recently. Derek showed her Rudy's picture. She frowned and said maybe she saw him a while ago but wasn't sure. They showed her Sawyer's picture and she had seen him in the area twice. It was just this week."

"Guess if the dead people carried any money with them, we now know where that money went. I'd say Sawyer found the empty cabin and took their cash for himself," said Jim.

"I think Sawyer figured out what happened and left. It's clear he knew these people and was well acquainted with them."

"So where did he go?"

Derek thought for a moment, "He went underground, probably still in the Los Angeles area."

They checked with the bait people and talked with a young kid. He told them about another couple who went fishing. He gave them their fake names.

They went back to the resort cabin owner who showed them the cabin the other couple rented. The people were nice and paid cash. The woman had gray hair and the man was blond. That's all he could remember. They looked normal. The building was one of his more expensive cabins and he hadn't rented it out yet. That's why he rented the place without checking their backgrounds. The owner unlocked the door.

Derek and Jim stepped in.

"Bleach. We have three burned candles in the kitchen, burned for some time. Good view through the window to our other cabin. We can see their parking space and their car without a scope."

"Have the police check out this cabin," said Derek. "But I doubt we will find anything. The garbage dumpsters were picked up a day sooner. Let's go to the boat rental."

The boat rental person showed them the high-powered speedboat that both couples rented.

"More bleach in one of the boats. Probably matches the bleach cabin. These people are pros. I bet their rental car is bleached as well," said Jim.

"Okay, have them check both boats. We'll probably find the deceased's fingerprints all over the other boat. Their fishing gear was back at the cabin. But there were no cell phones or cameras which is odd. The poisoner or poisoners probably took their real computers and cell phones for information. I'm sure they have dumped those objects."

"Yes, or fried them into scrap metal," warned Jim.

Derek shook his head. "What a waste? I think we are done."

The two men drove back to Los Angeles opting to stop at a barbeque place with homemade onion rings and margaritas some distance from the death zone. The thought of fish, hamburger, or beer wasn't too appealing to them.

30   Phoenix Race Announcers

TIM, THE ANNOUNCER came on, "Ladies and Gentlemen, welcome to the Phoenix Raceway in this glorious land. Don't you just love Arizona with all the prickly pears, saguaros, javelinas, and famous gunslingers? It is close to being in the land of Bora Bora again like when we were in Florida. I know some of our Bora Bora people are here today. Let's give a cheer."

The crowd cheered noisily. The Florida people golf on their vacations in Arizona. A person didn't have to replace their divots. The grass was so dry, there was no point to it.

Bill commented, "I read somewhere this state is definitely a wasteland. There was a cow skull with large horns outside my room. The dead thing looked like it was there for a long time. The paint underneath was clean. They hung the thing with barbed wire. The wire was the real stuff because it was rusty. You know there were steer on the range back in the wild west days when the real cowboys rode horses. I hear their posse here still rides horses with some cowboy leading the charge. They are really big suckers, the horses, I mean."

"We have our race guys riding their horses, Bill. They're just more protected now in their helmets, pads, roll cage, and special-engineered plastic or whatever they use for lightweight nowadays in those toy cars. All their gear is just like the pickers on those cactus, shiny and pointy. Every patch has a message and gets to the point. Shiny keeps the wild critters away and don't forget the fences. The race track has secure fences, so we won't get ambushed. The only thing we don't have is tunnels. The sheriff told me they closed ninety-four percent of them last week. The six percent is under those tall walls on the border. So, we're safe."

"Uh, huh," said Bill.

"Bill, are you with me? Pay attention. Did you know the penalties are high here in Phoenix? If any renegade accidentally bumps one of the sacred saguaros, the posse measures the penalty by the height of the cactus. Then there's the arms and white flowers on top of the cactus. Heaven forbid if there's critters in the sacred thing as the penalty count explodes out of sight."

"Are those flowers? I thought it was snow."

"No, that would be the cactus in Flagstaff, Bill."

Bill took out his map to locate the northern city.

"Long time ago the track here was dirt. Phoenix was the place to be then. There was no need for a tinted windshield back then. The dirt colored it well. But the cities in Arizona got together and told everyone there could be no more dust. You see the wives were tired of dusting the furniture all the time. Next you know it; they rolled out the tar, but the sand accidentally had some sea glass in it. The sand came from Davenport, California. Yes, there is one in California and Iowa, too. Heck, there could even be one in Washington. I digress a little. Getting back to the tar, they had to put a second layer on top around all the curves. The sparkle going around the corners was too distracting from the sea glass in the sand. The glare was like a woman walking in a low-cut sequin dress. The boys lost themselves every time."

"Besides, that's what I've been looking at in the stands. These Arizona women know how to kick it up a notch. They're afraid of nothing. Did you see all the bullet leather space holders on their belts? It was the exact size of a bullet. They are here to party. Even their flip flops have leather fringe and turquoise that sparkles."

The Arizona women in their audience stood up waving their cowboy boots and flip flops at the tower room.

Tim looked at Bill.

"Yeah, I met some of those women last night. A friend and I decided to follow the drivers who all know the hot spots in town. I think one of those places was a combination-hotel-casino. I just can't remember a thing after that drink out of the cowboy boot. I was so thirsty after those ten tacos. The label on the dish read: jalapeno cinco. What the heck is cinco? That's about the time I started to sink. She took her empty gun belt off and used it as a prop for my head. Oh, and then she warned me that she was a native from Scottsdale. Isn't Scottsdale a newer city? She invited me back and will show me her gun next time when we are hunting down the vortexes in Boynton Canyon in Sedona," said Bill.

"She sounds real nice. Isn't cinco Pig-Latin? No, I believe it's the number five. The dish you ate had five jalapenos? That's amazing you're still alive. However, you told me that guns were too dangerous. This woman sounds like danger. Or do the vortexes help?" asked Tim.

"That's what I'm hoping for. High excitement in a vortex. Oh, did you see the ears on those rabbits?"

Tim wondered why a grown man would be watching the bunnies. There were better things to be watching like the hawks. It was time to bring Bill back to the race track.

"I did. The ears sort of reminded me of the antennas on the pit crew chiefs. And, yes, they were also at the casino. I'm not sure if that's what you call fringe benefits, but those women were loaded in fringe. Maybe that's what made me dizzy. The swinging was awesome. It reminded me of those boys on the track squirreling around their tires when there's a red flag, and they must follow the pace vehicle."

Bill moved from rabbits to squirrels. He was thinking about the word danger, too. He said, "I'm glad we didn't stay at the teepee motel again."

"Why's that Bill? I thought it was loads of fun last year. They fed us real dead meat with green hot sauce. That hot sauce reminded me of a river I used to swim in. Man, that was good times."

"Naw, the teepee was too drafty at night and that glory racket from that hoot owl kept me up all night. He was following the pack of wolves that ran through. I could hear them fighting over my beef jerky I threw away or maybe it was the big sucker with the scorpion inside that I dropped in the dust."

The Arizona crowd cheered.

"Boy, that cheer is definitely for you. We love Arizona."

The crowd roared.

"All right, folks, our time is up. Sit back and relax with your peace pipes. What is it, Bill? Can't you see I'm busy?"

"Ah, the piece pipes are made in Colorado. I looked at the tag on one of them while we were in the store on Indian School Road."

Tim said, "I looked at the same peace pipe. It read on the card the information that the sandstone came from Colorado."

"Well, go figure that one out. The government must be out of control or what? There's plenty of sand here."

"Let's just watch out for the hot stuff in Arizona. There's no need to worry about the peace pipes. Well, I see the boys are ready, plus a few coyotes, and bobcats. Oops, sorry, I meant all you good looking driver critters are ready. I see the shiny sparkle from your uniforms and cars way up here. It's hard to contain all the crowd's excitement on these tracks. The engine exhaust is rising like a smoke signal. Maybe we are sitting on a vortex, Bill. The magic sea glass should help, kind of looks like a crystal. Anyway, don't you love this stadium and all the sponsors? Let's give everyone a hand before we exit."

The crowd clapped and whistled.

"Have a great run, boys. Hang tight around those degrees-of-something curves. When the green light flashes, just *Get Along Little Doggies.* See you later folks. I'm going to go get a heavy dose of espresso," said Tim.

It took a few minutes before the beer-garden crowd could contain themselves. The day was going to be another good race track afternoon. Tim handed the microphone to the real Commentator. Tim felt good because he was grinning. Another raging show just happened. Tim and Bill left the room heading for their garden sponsor.

31 Race and Proposal

MIC WAS UPSET. His race car was a little off, revving and choking up. He had not done well in the test run results. He was number eight in the startup line and Dan was number six. His carburetor throttle seemed to stick a little which meant acceleration big time. He didn't want to have to shut this engine down to stop this galloping horse from flying off the tracks. He felt the machine rev and he slipped around some of the curves hanging on tight.

Mic thought the announcer was correct in his assessment of rocks on the curves and the word, *Charge*. His car was a loose stallion outrunning the posse. The car was fully charged up like some living creature from an old west show. Mic told himself to get a grip. Or else, he would be out of this race shortly, i.e. in the wasteland.

He thought about Rudy and Sawyer. Then he thought about Alexa which was never a good thing to think about. He was angry that possibly Sawyer hurt her. He wanted to bash the guy's head in and that's why he snapped at his pit crew chief. The new air guns weren't working too well either. He was feeling the delay and stress. He would have to apologize to the chief later. He looked over at Frank in number seven position.

Frank was a nut case on the tracks. Mic would need to get around him from the beginning, but he worried more having the man on his back. He could throw him into a spin. Mic felt caged in. He told himself that it was just a race. He calmed himself down. He thought of Tiare.

The race started perfectly with the cars in sync for the first fifty laps and then the top ten took over the track leading the others. The top ten knew there were wannabe race car drivers ready to take over their position at any opportunity. The trick was to form a solid wall that they couldn't pass. They were experienced and did just that very thing for two hundred more laps. The large race track sign read forty-seven laps to go.

Mic was continuing to talk with his pit crew while racing. He talked to them about the performance of the tires and the car. His sponsor and manager were listening. They could see him driving the car delicately and then with full force when she slipped around the edges. Their main man was going to be tired at the end of this race.

"Hang in there, Mic, we are seeing the slippage. The car will be fixed, but not for this race. Do your best, okay."

"Okay. I will do."

Tiare saw Mic struggling with the car. Mic had talked to her about his racing experiences. She looked at Jim. He looked worried, because he saw it, too.

The light came on for a pit stop and all the race cars went into their pit areas for a fast change of tires and refueling. The pit chief talked to his manager and sponsors. We have massive wear on the left front tire.

"Are you hearing that, Mic?"

"Yes, I might have to come in early. How many tires left?"

"Just two."

"Then I'll try to ride them and do a little dance after the curves, so they wear evenly and make up for it on the straight away if things look clear. If not, I'll let the tires rub the corners on the turns."

"Check that. Good luck, Mic. We know you can do it. Just feel the track like you always do."

Mic would assess, recalculate, and drive this problem child across the line. All concentration was aimed at the car, driving, the competitors, the signals, his speed, and the glow of the tracks. Mic was transported into his world of racing. This car felt like his old man's truck driving around the back alleys. He knew he could bring the car in. He had driven worse.

Dan saw him in the rearview mirror and knew Mic was drag-racing this car home. He remembered their trip with the boar. "Think, hot sex, Mic."

Mic started laughing. Somehow, he saw Dan up ahead and felt the message.

Dan saw Mic pull alongside him. Mic gave the signal—Flipped out.

Dan stepped on his gas pedal to get himself out of Mic's space. Mic and his car was out of control. Tailing Dan, Mic saw his opportunity. This was the magic moment. He could make the race or not. Only a brave person would have made the next move. The sponsors would call it, go with the gut. Mic was all about stretching the boundaries. Mic was a gutsy-driver extraordinaire. He was perfection topped a notch. He was more than good.

Mic stepped on it through the straight away passing Frank's race car. Mic felt super and then he saw the two cars ahead hit the wall and each car dragging the other into a spin in front of him.

"Shit! Where is the safety zone? Think, man."

Mic's expertise at the track and racing junk cars led him to the sweet spot. He swerved to the left and re-righted the swinging. His car was moving back and forth in a dance narrowly missing the first damaged race car by two inches. The air swirling around his vehicle was trying to blow him into an accelerated spin.

Mic steered the car into a long slide and could feel his tires burn. He was steering his old man's truck.

"I am the person in control. There is no one else in this car, Mic"

The car steadied and magically the car picked up speed flying down to the next curve. Mic swung the corner wide, lightly rubbing the wall on the right side of his car so the side would look like crushed sea glass when he eventually crossed the finish line. The sparks were burning the metal. Mic felt the burning smell was a wasteland. The evil smell was super burnt-toast. This was not where he wanted to finish a race.

Finally, he drove the race car in his firm grip, hauling his vehicle down the tracks at amazing speed. Mic felt the car. He was one with his animal and both seemed to have turned into a piece of lightning. Then the lights went on and he slowed to enter the pit area. The beast was fighting him and wanted to continue the fight. He talked to his car and told the beast to wait. He was the master. The car pulled a hard right. Mic steered the vehicle secure in his gloved hands.

This was the last pit stop. His crew pulled off the tires. The tread was thirty percent gone on the left front tire, a little under that possibility on the other ones which was not a good zone to be in. Mic thought that was where the car performed perfectly. The stallion wanted to fly, untethered by rubber wheels. The car was ready to leave the dust. Mic let the beast roll. He was major behind. Tenth was not good enough. Mic talked to his machine.

"Let's do this."

Dan ended the race in fifth place and Mic landed in sixth place. Mic drove his car in to his pit crew to take care of it. The ride was a little too much today. Mic patted the animal car before he exited the scene. He turned over the stud car to them to fix. All he wanted was Tiare. He waved to Dan and walked past everyone.

His manager congratulated him. Mic only half heard him. He waved his sponsors off. He had only one focus. The focus was Tiare. He was ready. Mic couldn't let her escape from his life. He was determined when he saw her and ran. She was the only thing important. She was his music and love of his life. Mic ran like his life depended on her. Mic wasn't going to waste any more time. He had been there with women. He knew he was too slow this time. He thought of his crazy race car. There was a message there somewhere. Mic would be better at everything. He picked her up and swung her around. He loved feeling her body next to his. She was softness and memories. His mind clicked off the why of his feelings. She was the why to his life.

"Marry me, I love you."

"Yes," said Tiare. She had been waiting for this moment her whole life. His timing was perfect.

Dan saw them and knew something major was going down. He smiled. He already bought a new tux. He wondered where they would go for their honeymoon? He was sure it would be some place with Polynesian islands. Tiare told him about Mic's love song to her and he remembered the song at the restaurant while at the Wright and War Julio party.

Jess earlier informed Derek that she thought Mic would propose before he ever reached Fontana. Derek bet her a special dinner if she won. Jess was correct. She was good at speculation on things of the heart. But then, she was good at assessing criminals, too. She knew the bad ones would hold off, take a break, and appear in California.

32   Break at the Beach

TIARE TALKED WITH Jess about her engagement and wanted the news to remain a secret from the press. She needed Jess to design her bridesmaid dresses and her wedding gown. Jess was ecstatic and found them a place to stay for the weekend.

The location was Jack and Ara Jones' home on the beach near Laguna and Dana Point. Jack and Ara were touring Europe for a month. Mic and Tiare would stay in their elegant guest bedroom. Mic would have access to a room of expensive exercise equipment.

Jess met them there and left some designs for Tiare to review. She brought a special book that was the collection of her wedding gowns. Jess drew different island creations for the bridesmaid dresses and something super grand for Tiare. She hugged Mic and Tiare and left them. Jess had stocked the refrigerator with champagne, a wonderful chef-prepared dinner, bread, eggs, sausage, and orange juice for breakfast. There was a fruit basket and fresh bouquet of flowers on the table. The bar was fully stocked. She moved the cleaning lady's routine to work the house Tuesday after the guests were gone.

The couple were scheduled to visit the Diamond Exchange building for one of Jess's favorite jewelers. He created custom rings. Tiare wanted something in a pear shape that was huge. Mic called the shape, the rock. He was no fool when it came to women. It was always that old saying, "A diamond can never be big enough." He would buy her good enough and big enough.

Mic checked out the beach house upon arrival.

"Come here, love."

Tiare grinned. She was anxious to look at the bridesmaid dresses and he knew it. She did a little dance around him. He grabbed her and hauled her into the bedroom. Then he came back out to get the basket with the champagne glasses which were inscribed with their names. He took the cooled champagne and went into their guest room. The pictures could wait a little.

Tiare knew the dance would entice Mic. He could hardly stop touching her on the drive from the airport in Ontario to the Jones' home. Mic forgot the strawberries and raced back to get them out of the refrigerator.

"You are the sweetest person. How did you know that I needed a strawberry?" She slowly sucked on it and didn't take a bite. She fed it to Mic who ate half. She ate her half as he slowly kissed her. Mic made love to his fiancé just the way she liked. Her lips tasted good and he wanted more. They snuggled in bed the rest of the afternoon. Finally, they were getting hungry. They showered together in their huge marble bathroom and got dressed. Mic started the outside grill. He peeked in the containers earlier and read the chef's directions.

Mic was good at grilling and placed their thick steaks on the end. The baked potatoes and the sweet corn wrapped in foil were placed in the back. There was a foil packet of cotija cheese butter to drip on the corn after cooking. He was glad there was a top warming rack to finish the Elote. He put the container of sauce and savory butter there along with the cooked prosciutto-wrapped asparagus. The outdoor meal shouldn't take but eight to twelve more minutes.

Tiare came out with their mixed drinks. Oh, good, they have a two-person hot tub on their deck. We can jump in and watch the stars after we look at the bridesmaid dresses. I'll look at the bridal gowns when you are exercising tomorrow.

"So, I can't see your gown tomorrow?"

"No, you don't want bad luck."

"That's not true, the bad luck part?"

"I'm not sure, but I don't want to risk it. Besides, I want you dazed when you see me."

"I'm already a little dazed. How much more dazed and off the rocker can I get?"

She hit him on the arm gently.

"Oow. Not really. How do you like your steak?"

"Medium."

"Medium, the dead meat is. I thought you Miami women liked things raw, eating alligator and all. Or is it boar?"

She raised her hand to hit him again and he grabbed her and kissed her.

"This beach place is fun. Maybe we should buy one. Where do you want to live, by the way? We haven't really talked about our life together and then there are children. How about twelve of the little things. We'd be a fully loaded racing team with pit crew."

"I like both Miami and Los Angeles. Maybe we can buy a home in one place and a condominium on the beach in the other. Oh, and only one or two children, please. Otherwise, we'd need two more buses."

"Sounds fine with me." Mic and Tiare finished their dinner, placed any dishes in the dishwasher, and leftovers in the refrigerator.

"Promise me something."

"Yes, what is it, Mic?"

"If I get too much sometime, you'll let me know, right?"

"Yes, love, you will be the first to know. However, will you listen?"

Tiare thought about the people she had been surrounded with most of her life. They were high-ego and high-oriented toward advancement. Triple achievement was where the men resided. Mic seemed normal to her or, rather, a high-normal.

"Besides, I like having things set at the too-much scale. Too much triple-A personality and sex are working for me."

Mic grinned. He started kissing her.

"Oh, no, no, we have pictures waiting."

"Okay, let's do this," said Mic because Tiare had this look on her face. It's the look she gave criminals.

Tiare grinned back and took his hand. Opening the book, they sat down close together on the large sectional couch and looked at the bridesmaid dresses.

The choices were amazing and hard to select just one, but they finally selected the same dress. The dress was a black strapless long chiffon gown, form-fitted, and gathered below the waist with peach and champagne embroidered flowers. The flowers were like garlands which trailed from the top down into swirls to the bottom.

The design flowed well and would fit their Polynesian theme. The girls would love the dresses and they would go with the black and champagne satin platform heels she had chosen for them. The men would wear black tuxedos, white shirts, and champagne cummerbunds. Tiare was pleased.

She could hardly wait to view her dress drawings. Jess told her about one of the dresses and the massive white pearls in the design. There also was included with the dress a design for a headdress of white pearls and white feathers.

They went for a walk on the beach because Mic's bodyguard finally arrived. The man missed his flight. Mic and Tiare were safe because Derek had sent a bodyguard to the house and to the airport. Derek's bodyguard stayed with them for the weekend as well. There was a room over the garage to accommodate both men who enjoyed the life at the beach home.

Mic and Tiare enjoyed their break at the beach. After selecting their diamonds and ring designs, they played in the surf, getting sunburned. After the hot tub, they rubbed aloe gel on each other at the end of the day. No one recognized them on the beach. They wore hats with sunglasses and looked like the other babes with their jock boyfriends. They were part of the young crowd of tourists.

Tiare reviewed the wedding dress designs and sent Jess an email. She wanted number twenty-five with the headdress. She would have to change her flowers to white phalaenopsis orchids. Jess left a space for them on the headdress and annotated that on the design. The dress was wow-factor big time. The headdress was what she wanted. Mic would be speechless when he saw her in the dress. She went online once again and ordered her satin and clear plastic heels with red and white soles.

Mic and Tiare used up the whole bottle of aloe that weekend. Their bedroom door was forever shut. Jess had left them menus of her favorite takeout and delivery restaurants close by. Their bodyguards flipped a coin and one or the other one picked up some of the meals, so they could see sane people and not the two lovers all the time.

Jess bought them flip flops and large yellow beach towels in case they forgot theirs. There were two yellow rubber duckies for the hot tub with a raft. She wanted them to have a grand time. She and Derek left them alone. The weather was perfect, balmy, filled with sunshine, and more than ever blue-sky days.

Mic told Tiare the record company was set to release his first actual recorded song in a deal with his friend. She was delighted. They wouldn't release the song until after the California race. Mic hoped the bad people would be caught soon.

33   Wedding Dress Correction

JESS RECEIVED A call from her marketing representative that one of their well-to-do customers was unhappy about her gown and wanted to speak with her about changes to make the dress a more custom design. Jess agreed to meet with them at Johann's Restaurant in Los Angeles. She thought it would be all right because Derek had not yet returned from a different project he was pursuing. She took her bodyguard with her.

Upon arriving early at the restaurant, they waited ten minutes for the client to arrive. Jess was surprised to see that it was Melissa Grainger, the young woman engaged to the politician. It was the politician whose wife was murdered a short time ago. Jess looked at her marketing representative who didn't seem surprised at all. She should have asked the client's name. The error was too late to back out now.

Jess was introduced and proceeded to work with the young woman on a change to the dress. They removed the shoulder ruffle and inserted a new fan pleat that Jess created. The new simple draft drawing was completed. Jess showed her some samples of the fabric and how well it went with her other dress fabric. The fan design would lay down closer to the body than the ruffle and worked well with the snug dress curvature and the woman's figure. Melissa signed the contract for the change and was now happy with her dress or would be shortly. Jess's manufacturer would work up the new look and her marketing representative could contact Melissa when it was completed. Jess was done with her appointment and stood up to leave. She wouldn't need to meet with Melissa again.

There was a flurry by the door and the politician entered the restaurant. He came directly over to his fiancée's table. He kissed her and sat down.

"Hello, Mrs. Wright. It's nice to see you again, only up close this time. You were at the Edwards graduation ceremony except we must have just missed you. Please sit down, I would like to see your design," said Rich Madden.

Jess sat back down and showed the politician the new design with Melissa's approval.

"Perfect. This is exactly what my baby needs, something very custom so she will shine on our special day."

"I'm glad you like the design, but I really must leave. I have a busy schedule today," said Jess.

As she stood up, she saw the strange woman in a black one-piece designer jumpsuit and wedge heels enter the restaurant. The maître de escorted the woman to a table across from the politician and his fiancé. Jess looked worriedly at her bodyguard who nodded that he was ready anytime she wanted to leave. Jess hugged her marketing representative goodbye at the door to the restaurant and looked back at the strange woman with strawberry blonde hair. She was approximately twenty-five or twenty-six years old and very pretty. Something bothered her about the woman. Jess frowned and left the restaurant.

She and her bodyguard walked across the street when Jess thought of an idea, and they entered the coffee shop across from the departed restaurant. While her bodyguard ordered their coffee lattes, she watched the restaurant front door. The politician and his fiancé left the restaurant. The woman in the jumpsuit came out. Jess took several pictures of the woman as she crossed the street to get into her car. The woman was so focused on following the politician that she didn't see Jess.

The camera was used again to catch the license plate as the woman sped away. Jess stepped back from the window as the woman turned around to look behind her. It was as if she knew that someone was suddenly watching her. The woman pulled over and got out of her car. The red-haired woman looked toward the coffee shop.

That's when Jess and her bodyguard high-tailed it through the back door and into the alley to another boutique store that Jess knew. The back of the boutique store was open, because a new shipment of dresses arrived. They ducked into the shop. The men blocked the back door with the dress racks until they could close it. Jess didn't want the woman to see her, especially when she was suddenly the subject of the woman's focus.

She talked to her bodyguard as they walked to their vehicle. She didn't want him to report this part of her day to Derek. She would talk to Derek privately. The bodyguard knew Derek would not be pleased with him, but the lady of the house also signed his paycheck. He would be on her side in this one. There was something off at the restaurant.

34   Pictures of Tracker

DEREK ARRIVED IN the San Diego parking lot and told his security people that he had arrived. One of his security team escorted him to his yacht. Jess had been informed and was waiting for him in the outside bar area.

"Honey, there you are. I'm happy to be home."

Derek bent down and kissed her cold scotch-tasting lips which were coral-colored. He smiled. Derek remembered the Tomales Bay bar when he kissed her there. Dream girl sitting in a bar was the only thing he saw that day. He always liked to kiss her. She wore one of her short, casual sundresses with heeled sandals. They were both a hot coral color. She wore a twinkle in her eye. Her long blonde hair was pulled back into a ponytail with a gold band. He wondered where she found that one. There was a gold seahorse swinging with her tail of hair. The trinket would be gone shortly. Derek planned on it landing somewhere else.

Jess looked at her handsome husband. "Hi, honey, how was your day?"

Derek knew that something good happened today. Or at least something important that she wanted to tell him.

"Where is everyone?"

"Justin, our son, is staying with his rock band friend and Sami, our daughter, is staying with Rhonda, Skid, and Maggie. They are off to a new show that the girls absolutely must see. The twin girls, Cata and Alina, are with Jack and Ara. They are going to the zoo tomorrow with their daughter, Lis. We are finally all alone for an evening."

"Great, that's a perfect ending to my day, a lovely time with my beautiful wife who I am very fond of every day."

"Thank you." Jess kissed him again.

"I asked the chef to make salad and clam chowder tonight. We can have a quick meal. He made your corn muffins with the honey butter. I need to let you know about my day."

"The food sounds good. What's up?"

"There was a client that I met today who wanted to change their wedding gown. We met at our favorite lunch restaurant downtown with my marketing representative. As we were leaving the client, her fiancé arrived. Guess who her fiancé was that we also met?"

"I have no clue."

"It was the politician, Rich Madden, and the soon-to-be-bride is Melissa Grainger."

Derek's eyes went dark and he ran his hands through his hair.

"We talked about this man and I asked you specifically to stay away from him."

"Yes, I was surprised to see him and hadn't really planned on doing so. My marketing representative will handle all future communications with Melissa."

Derek sipped his drink, "Good, I don't want you anywhere near him, not until we figure out what happened to his wife."

"I will stay away, but there is something else."

Derek frowned and look worried. There was that one word again. "What something else?"

"Our politician, Mr. Madden, is being followed by a woman." Jess pulled up her pictures on her cell phone and scrolled through them for Derek. She didn't show him the last photo.

"I don't recognize her at all," responded Derek.

Jess looked contemplative. "Remember when I was at the Napa Jewelry store the night of the robbery? I felt strange, like there was a scary and bad person watching me."

Now Derek looked concerned, "And you felt that same way today when you saw this woman tracking our suspect, Madden."

"Yes."

"What are you thinking? The family of the dead wife have hired no investigator because I checked on those facts with them. We know the woman was not an investigator, private or otherwise. The politician may have other enemies, or it could have been a member of the press."

Jess knew her idea was a reach, even for Derek, but she had to tell him. "The woman kept the politician in front of her. In other words, the man didn't see her. She was keeping out of his direct line of sight. The hidden agenda of the woman was uncanny. What if we have a member of Snake woman's team tracking the politician?"

"Why would she authorize that? It can't be the same woman the police have in the photo because this woman is too young. Snake woman has been on the circuit for a long time and should be in her late forty's."

"Exactly. Perhaps this person is quietly doing some outside research first. If it was Snake woman, the politician would be dead by now. Maybe this woman doesn't have permission to kill yet. What if this woman is related somehow to the Snake woman or is someone highly-favored among her employees? Notice that there is no tattoo around her neck. Therefore, she is not one of the copycats. If she doesn't have permission from the Snake woman, she could feel constrained by the Snake woman. I know that I'm throwing theories out into the open, but we need to look at things differently. These people change their game too fast. We have got to be faster."

Derek ran his hands through his hair again. He knew not to tell his wife that she was heavily into speculation. Yet, the more he thought about her words, some items made sense.

"The photo and your story seem a little bit impossible. Why would she want to kill the fiancée or the politician? They have not crossed her that we are aware of. The fiancée is someone new to the scene. There is only a slight connection for Madden which might be Miami."

Jess nodded, "But we usually run into the impossible and more-than-possible scenarios. Perhaps we have a power-play situation with a younger version wanting control of the house. The woman wore a mean look when she was watching the politician. She wasn't interested in the fiancée. The woman was clenching her hands like someone constrained and angry. The look was one of super hatred and control."

She showed him the last picture.

Derek smiled, "Good girl. You're right. She does have a strange hatred look with her compressed mouth and squinting eyes. See how her hands have scrunched the heavy menu back. The word that comes to my mind is tense. She was very close to the man and was controlled. I hope she didn't see you take this photo or the other ones."

"I don't think so, because she was almost hyper-focused on following the politician. After she left the restaurant, her behavior returned to the stalking mode. Then she turned toward my direction as if she felt my presence. The woman pulled her car over and stopped to look back at the coffee house. We were inside the heavy dark glass part of the window. That's when we quickly exited the coffee shop, stepped out the back door, and walked into my favorite boutique for a little bit."

"Jess, I wish you would not do crazy stuff. I don't need any tracker person focusing on you. This is too dangerous."

Jess laughed, "Yes, I know you don't like the crazy stuff. I'm used to danger. It's what you do for a living. What was it you used to say? I believe it was something about being freaking nuts. I will try to stay as far away from the scary woman, and I don't care to run in to her at all. If I do, you will be the first person that I call. That is before I fire up my bomb, throw it toward her vehicle, and run. But you do like the photos? I did see you smile. What will you do with them?"

"Yes, I recall the word, nuts and please, no fire bombs on cars or outside tanks."

Derek reached over and gave her a kiss. He liked her just the way she was, crazy and everything else and she knew it. She was the only person he cared to go that route.

"I'm glad that you will call me. You do that move much better now that we are married. I don't know about the rest of the what part. I'm not sure that I want to give the photos to the police just yet because it would be obvious that you took them. I don't think the politician is in danger for now. Maybe they want him to marry and feel secure. Then they can take everything from him like he did his wife. The woman following him is interesting. I don't believe the politician, or his security saw her either. They seem bored and oblivious in a few of your photos. For now, we wait. I don't want someone to leak the photos from the police and into the Snake woman's hands either. She has contacts everywhere. The discovery of these photos could change the timing and our ability to locate her. The tracker woman in the photos could become our useful link to the bigger game."

Derek sighed. He had wanted a quiet evening with his wife. He was tired of figuring out the bad guy's game. He needed another break.

"Let me think about this one. I will show our team, however. We can trace the rental car, but I doubt she still has it. I'll ask Brandon to check the license plate. If the vehicle's been bleached inside the rental car, we will know we have a potential suspect for the Big Bear Lake murders. There could be a second member of her team as there existed a woman and man at the second cabin on the lake. You didn't see him and perhaps he wasn't there. Let's hope he wasn't. They probably switch off following their prey, one during the day and the other at night."

The chef brought their dinner. Derek looked at Jess and shook his head. It was impossible to protect his wife. But tonight, was going to be a respite. He winked at her and wished he had picked up a bouquet of flowers for her. He would be surprised entering their bedroom because she already bought the flowers, champagne, and dessert of double-fudge brownies. She also checked the temperature on their hot tub. Their towels and swimsuits were waiting. Jess knew that he needed to be alone with her.

Derek ate his soup and looked at her half bowl. He loved clam chowder. She was eating her salad and saw him. She passed him her partial soup bowl. He dug into the second bowl. Jess laughed. They always shared their dinner. They shared everything now. There was no need for any distance or difficult truces. He passed her the cracker basket. They were on the same side. Jess picked up the stereo remote and hit their favorite number six calypso song.

"This is going to be a private evening," said Derek.

"Very private."

He knew that the gods were with him. Derek laughed. He knew there was more. There always was more.

35   Rudy Sees Sawyer

RUDY FOUND HIMSELF a part-time job at the Santa Monica food kitchen for the indigent souls. He found some newer, hand-me-down clothes, and worked also part-time at a local exercise place taking out garbage and mopping the floor. At night, he hid in the locker area until everyone left and then he stayed overnight sleeping on some stacked yoga mats. He always snuck out when a few people arrived at the club. He saved his money in a secret bankroll under his shirt in case he needed to run.

Trent Rudy came out of the food kitchen and dodged back inside as he watched Sawyer stroll by the open door. His own beard and hair were long as a new disguise, but he must be careful. Rudy squeezed himself behind a flag and stand, hiding himself in the kitchen. Then he raced to the door and grabbed his old hat with sunglasses. He tailed Sawyer to a sandwich shop, and then he turned around. Sawyer was walking back toward him. Rudy hid again and was behind a garbage dumpster in the alleyway. After Sawyer passed, he followed the man back to a decrepit apartment.

"Why was Sawyer in California? How long has he been in town? The upcoming Fontana race weekend was almost here, of course. I'll need to see if there is a bus that travels there, and I'll have to ask a co-worker to get me a ticket for the races that Dan and Mic participate in."

Tracker woman saw both men. She was dressed in drag today to blend into the crowd of people walking to and from work. She followed Sawyer into the library and saw him sit down by the computer area. He had done the computer search every day for the past week. When he stood up and left, she went to the computer and saw the same website.

"He's going to the Fontana race. The next race was Sawyer's computer obsession."

She was told to eliminate the man by Max for Snake woman. The elimination must be an accident. Max emphasized those commands. There were to be no drugs at all. Max explained to her that Sawyer was connected to the two dead copycats at Big Bear Lake. Snake woman wasn't sure how much information Sawyer was told about her operation. She couldn't risk leaving him alive. Snake woman knew the man killed the rich socialite named Alexa.

No loss to the world. It would be her pleasure to do the police a small favor this one little time. Sawyer sealed his fate when he consorted with the Burrows who were copycats stealing from her. The Snake woman also thought the Burrows killed her dear friend Matin Domingo while he was in jail. The Burrows paid the price for stealing and killing her friend. It was now Sawyer's turn. His death would be unkind.

Tracker frowned. She was successful in convincing Max about the Burrows' unworthiness.

There was one small item that was a lie. She didn't correct Max. She couldn't divulge this small piece. It was a small thing except she knew Snake woman's temper. There was no way she was going to divulge her error in judgment and get caught in the ringer. Snake woman would put her down in a heartbeat. It wouldn't matter that she was partial family.

Then there was the other item no one knew about. The other item had to do with the yellow sports car. The Tracker wished she never purchased the thing in Germany from an underground dealer. The car was never registered in her name. She gave the car to her lover. The car was gone, in pieces and parts, so she was safe. The photos on her old computer had been deleted. The computer was given to a priest in a nearby church. There was no way anyone could find the computer or connect her. The old computer began nagging at her brain. She should contact the priest to see if he still owned the computer. Maybe she could trade and give him a new one. The photos were on the hard drive still. Tracker made a stupid mistake giving her computer away. Then she remembered one photo that was printed and placed inside the yellow car door.

There was murder work to be done in Fontana. The German priest could wait. New plans must be made here. The Tracker used a bus before to delay the man to a previous race. It would be easy to pick him up again. The kill on a bus would work. The timing of the arrival of the bus would be the hard part. She would put an ad in the paper for the bus that would take people directly to the game for a fee. Then she could drop her patrons close to the stadium. Tracker would kill him on the return trip. Sawyer would be the only one who would know the return departure time. Everyone else would be told an earlier time. A second bus would pick up the other people. He would have his own special trip with only one other occupant and the bus driver.

Her hookup person for the buses and necessary permits was contacted. The Tracker's partner would drop the newspaper off at the decrepit apartment building to make sure Sawyer read the ad. Her partner would set up the cell phone connection. He would hire actors and actresses for the first trip to the race. Those people would have to take the earlier bus or find another way home. The pickup location for Sawyer was a couple blocks from his apartment. The spot would be the same place she picked him up before. Her bus uniform was ready.

She called Max. "Everything's ready for Sawyer. What about Madden?"

Max was getting tired of her asking the same question about the politician. "The answer is still the same. The answer is no."

"I believe she is getting soft."

"It is not up to you to understand her. I must remind you. Your job is to follow instructions and I might add, to the letter."

Tracker was getting anxious to move on the second job. She didn't like the delay. She hated him, the politician. The politician was worst scum than Sawyer. He had no authority to still be living in her books.

"I will hold but I don't like this. The man is a major problem for women. We know he killed his wife from the photos the Burrows couple took, and the blackmail note they sent to Madden. The money, Madden's family money, was in their bags along with the other money. His Miami family paid for him. He couldn't even pay the money himself. In the note, he told the Burrows he was getting married and couldn't afford any more funds to disappear out of his accounts. He whined that his fiancée was spending money hand-over-fist for the wedding. The Burrows were going to still squeeze him for money. We did the politician a favor. It's just that the police are still unaware of those items and facts. We have the information in our possession. It's stupid, not her, but the situation is."

Max felt the stubbornness rear in the Tracker. "You can have the opportunity to talk to her when we've completed a few more assignments. Make sure you stay under cover. We don't need advertising at this point of your location or our involvement. You will wait and follow my orders. If she knew you were arguing with me, the Snake woman would be displeased. I have kept our discussions to a minimum about your attitude."

"I am always careful. You don't need to remind me. My attitude is fine."

Max heard her belligerence and needed to leave. "Keep it that way because she asked for your careful preparation specifically. Also, stay away from policemen, investigators, and their wives."

Tracker was now more frustrated. She wished she hadn't mentioned Mrs. Wright in her report. She had toyed with the idea quite heavily. The Tracker saw Jess at the restaurant only. She downed one of her stay-calm pills. Then she took a second one. The pills didn't seem to help anymore. It wasn't her fault Mrs. Wright was a designer in wedding dresses and the designer of the politician's fiancée.

She was mad and drove by the police station on purpose. Then Tracker pulled over and went into a sandwich shop where she knew the police liked to eat. It made her feel better. She walked out with her turkey meatball sandwich and soda. Today, she wore tourist clothes and a baseball hat.

She picked up the bus uniform from the drycleaners for her partner. Then she pulled into a fast food gas station and purchased new rubber gloves and bleach. She bought a foot-long hotdog and potato chips for him. "This stuff will kill a person for sure." She had the clerk put the food in two bags. She didn't have to smell the meat in the vehicle.

Next, she stopped at a clothing store. She purchased a few clothes and several small backpacks to set the stage for the bus trip with Sawyer.

36 Fontana Preparation

MIC AND TIARE pulled into the parking lot where his racing motorhome was assigned a slot at the Fontana Raceway. Mic opened the door and helped her up the steps into his strong arms.

"We're home, love. It feels good to be back here."

"Yes, it does. This is truly who you are, isn't it?"

"I am the entire complete race package," said Mic.

"And my powerhouse. I wish we had a little time to snuggle but I have a meeting with my team."

"Tell everyone hello for me. Ask them to catch Sawyer, because I'm tired of looking over my shoulder worrying about his dirty tricks. I believe Dan and I are so done with the disturbance in our space."

"I'll do that. Let's hope they have new information," mentioned Tiare. She kissed him and left the motorhome.

Mic dressed in his gear and went down to the garage to talk with his bosses. He was scheduled to drive the track and looked forward to feeling the raceway under his tires again. He waved to Dan who shook his head in a nod. Entering his vehicle for the timed run, Mic heard the Showmen come on over the raceway speaker system. He laughed, because he always drove better when they were around.

"Hello, ladies and gentlemen, here are the Showmen, Tim and Bill, to entertain us today."

Tim picked up the microphone, "What state did you say we were in, Bill?"

"I think we passed the windmills sometime during the night, but I'm not real sure. We're possibly in California."

"Crowd, where are we?"

Everyone yelled, "Fontana."

"Oh, yeah, the fun in the sun, Fun-Tana. Well, it's good to be here and get away from the cat."

Bill frowned, "What's wrong with your cat?"

"Oh, about one o'clock in the morning, she zooms around our master bedroom and becomes a hell-cat like she was in some bumper car race and the top pole thing was throwing sparks at her. Perhaps I should call her pole-cat for the number of pole wins she has gotten lately. I should probably penalize her for going too fast on the pit road. I mean the exit ramp. Then I found the catnip mouse that my wife bought her at a clearance sale. It explained everything happening in that bedroom. Speaking of bumper cars, I bet those boys down there in the pits went to the local fair like we did and drove those insanely, unsafe, silly things. It was child's play in the land of demolition derby time. Weren't the walls wood or was it killer metal?"

"The walls were cheap, dented metal. You know the race boys went to the fair because they are too young to have been whiskey runners. That was the good times when the windows on the big long cars were rounded. The round windows distribute the stress from the air making the cars go airborne with those powerful engines. We can't do that now. No sir, airborne is out the door at the race track. Speaking of power, didn't we own it? I remember the time we took Jake to that noisy bumper car place. He was the guy with those dorky, dark-rimmed glasses, but we didn't mind them. We knew the fair people fixed those bumper cars and disconnected the rod from the steering wheel on some of them just to confuse us. Or maybe it was to slow us down like those restrictor plates do," said Bill.

"That's right, I remember, we had been there at the bumper car ride before. We knew which cars the duds were. We brought wax and polished those dud cars up real shiny. Then we put stickers on them from our favorite sponsors. What was on some of those stickers? Oh, now it's coming clear, pardon me, but I had a brain moment from too much toxin from my dermatologist visit. One sticker said Princess Piss Beer Company and the other one said Hot Dog from the Coon Hound Company. That's the car Jake drove, and we bumped him around the track for over an hour. We told him there probably wasn't enough lug nuts and that's why his wheels popped into the wall. The amazing thing is the guy believed us. Did you see any lug nuts or racing tires on those bumper cars?"

"That was fun. Jake couldn't win at anything. He drove his car kind of squirrely, too, when we waved the yellow flag. Wasn't that first one sticker some beer company from Wisconsin or Iowa? I didn't know you were going to a dermatologist. I thought only the ladies did that."

Tim laughed, "No, I think the beer was from Michigan or maybe Canada. It said north pole something. I see the dermatologist because I need to look handsome as I get older. It's important to look like a winner. I got a permanent once, but it didn't work with the cat. She wouldn't talk to me for a week. My other half-blind, half-dead cat who sleeps all day came alive and did lots of talking. The second cat reminded me of an old girlfriend that I had. She wouldn't be quiet either. But then we are used to all the noisy women at the track. Let's hear it, girls; say right on."

The women in the crowd shouted, "Right on!"

"I'm glad the women are with us today. You scared me when you mentioned an old girlfriend. Did you hear they caught the RV bandit in Daytona? I'm real glad about that bust. The man stole my wallet out of my friend's RV. My friend and I were at the tracks when the bandit was there. I can't imagine why he didn't take my watch?"

"That's real terrible. Did you lose much money?" asked Tim.

"Naw, the wife already took my one credit card and there was only four dollars in the wallet. The driver's license was an easy fix to replace and, of course, my grocery card. The watch was plastic."

"Yes, I can see the bandit throwing your identification card away. No one has a mug like yours. But he probably used your gas miles from the grocery card. Now that's too bad. Those miles are valuable. The plastic watch didn't have the app capability so that makes sense why he didn't want it."

"Yeah, I had over 100 points on the grocery card. They have watches that use apps? I didn't know that. My birthday is coming up soon. Thanks."

"Maybe that's why those RV people beat him up before the police could intervene. It must have been a sore point, the watches that the bandit stole were everything. I can see what lit those RV boys up. Anyway, shouldn't we be talking about the race car boys about now before we have to leave?" asked Tim.

"Oh, right. Let me take a sip of my drink," mentioned Bill.

"How did you get beer? Did those RV boys give you some? I hear they hide keggers in their haul trailers. Oh, I see, Bill. You put the drink in your aluminum flask. It's the one with the wheel design and winner's flags on the side. Did you forget you put the beer in there last night? We were at the hotel after we drove by those windmills?"

"Sorry, I did forget. I do remember the windmills. There were miles of them spinning. It drove me a little crazy. That's why my minds not working today. There was something in the air that must be contagious. It's a new disease called brain failure. This morning I decided to be a changed man and put mint tea in my flask."

Tim looked at Bill. "I've heard of that illness. There's absolutely no cure other than mint. Mint was a good idea." Tim sipped the iced tea.

"Speaking of contagious, there's been lots of love happening around us. You know that I got hitched to the little lady from Scottsdale."

The crowd whistled and clapped for Bill.

"Thank you everyone. Well, it's time to spill more peace and love news. We've been told by a secret spy that there is a marriage proposal on the table for one of our favorite race car drivers, but I was told to keep it a secret."

Tim frowned, "We are on the air, you know, unless you're still in brain failure mode."

Bill laughed, "The brain has recovered. It was the mint that killed the capsaicin that stuck to the bottom of the flask from the Bloody Mary you drank before. I'm going to drop hints to the crowd about the upcoming marriage. People pay attention to those juicy tidbits of information. See, the heads have turned to look at our tower. People have stopped eating their cheese pretzels. They love secrets. Secrets win over pretzels. We'll make all these fans come back next month when we are in Talladega, just so they can hear the good news."

"Aah, Talledega. The track seems to have strong vortexes on the whole surface, but I'm not sure if they are the right kind. I felt a little lift when we parked the car in the Alabama lot," said Tim.

"I know, there's a lot of lift on that raceway. The car lifts, rolls, and the roof scrapes the spectator fences. One car is going airborne, flying perpendicular to the ground, rolling a few times, touching one car, then another. It's the same bumper car reaction we had at the fair. Then there's always a race car that starts on fire. The smell of burning, smoking tires and brake pads control the air space."

"I remember those wrecked thirty-five cars out of forty that one year. How much money wasted was that? Five hundred thousand times thirty-five is over seventeen million if a person had to do a total replacement. But most of these garage guys work wonders with the damaged vehicles. The tracks that day looked like Louie's Used Junkyard with pieces and parts everywhere. The tracks were quite a show and we are always glad when the drivers exit those vehicles safe. The vortex there was only dangerous, thankfully, to the cars. But, Bill, nothing ever happens at Fontana. This is a calm place and rarely has any lift around the tracks. The breeze is only around those windmills."

"Good, because I'm going to relax. It's time to roll."

Tim looked at Bill. "Don't say that word, roll. You might stir things up and open a door to the vortex."

"Oh, no."

Tim responded, "Have a great run today, boys. Enjoy the Fontana sunshine because we hear there will be some temporary rain shortly. I believe they call them mini-bursts. The weather people told us that it will probably be just enough to wet the pavement. I understand the winner of the race gets a choice of a case of champagne from California or a whole year's worth of dates. Or was it artichokes? We love eating those baby artichokes fried in heavenly batter and dipped in pizza sauce near Gilroy."

Bill stood up. "It doesn't matter just so it wasn't garlic."

Tim was convinced it was time to exit. First, he must do one last assignment. "Let's hear it for all those wineries and flavored water companies sponsoring the race today."

The California crowd roared.

"That's a wrap everyone. I'm going to Laguna and buy my wife some sea glass jewelry."

37 Fontana Race Day

MIC WAS HAPPY that he obtained the number five slot and Dan was in number eight. The race started, and the tires were new. The drivers were ready to hurl their wonder machines down the tracks. It was a good race for over one hundred fifty laps, then there was a little fallout. One vehicle tagged another, and the cars scrambled to surge around the five stalled cars and the yellow flag slowed them down. Mic and Dan held onto their places. All the vehicles drove in for the pit stop.

Sawyer already entered the garages earlier as a manufacturer's rep. He stole the uniform, badge, and box from the real person. Sawyer tracked him for a week. The man didn't even lock his house. Sawyer went inside and found what he needed in the basement to subdue him. He tied the man up with duct tape and left him in his basement. Then he punctured his tires and put his cell phone in a dumpster.

It was easy to exchange out the lug nuts for a box of defective ones in Dan and Mic's area. Sawyer felt good. Everything went smooth for him with the man's truck and entrance past security. The police and the two drivers wouldn't know what jolt hit them when their tires fell off. He could just envision the wheel-hop crash.

Sawyer looked at his watch. The time was right for him to meet the bus. He decided not to chance using the manufacturer's truck. He was walking to the bus pickup spot when he saw a man that he knew. He looked different, but he could smell the pipe tobacco. It was Trent Rudy and he wanted to catch him to see if he could con him into a drink. He didn't know Rudy knew that Sawyer wanted to kill him at Big Bear Lake. Sawyer thought his cover was still intact with Trent Rudy. He would get Rudy to meet him for a drink later, too. Then Sawyer would kill him because he knew too much.

Sawyer called out to the man who looked in horror at him. Rudy started running. That's when Sawyer knew he had to fix his other problem. Sawyer ran after his man. Trent Rudy ran in front of the bus which seemed to slow a little. Rudy had dropped his hot dog and beer in the paper bag at the curb in his haste to leave the area. Sawyer saw the bus rolling toward him and thought he could make it across in time. Next, Sawyer tripped on the paper bag.

The bus picked up speed and seemed to lift a little off the ground. A dark cloud formed in the upper atmosphere and was heavy laden with moisture. The bus was heading directly at Sawyer who turned to look at the bus. It was the same bus driver and the old guy that he saw in Miami. Sawyer wondered how that phenomena could be true. Then he realized who the two people were inside the bus. It was the woman in a boat at Big Bear Lake.

The two people were the man and woman in the cabin. They were the Snake woman's trackers. The door of the bus was open and then it closed. The whole brain fired the message, they were the murderers of his friends, the Burrows. At the same time, he saw the upper sign on the bus. In horror, he read the word on the digital bus marque as it flipped from *Expired* to *Deadman*.

The bus slowed even though the driver pressed his foot to the gas. The woman and driver looked at the gas gage. It appeared to be empty. In their rush, they failed to gas up. The woman drew her gun with the silencer. The bus slowed, and Sawyer jumped up to grasp onto the windshield wiper to avoid being run over. He saw the woman with the gun and struggled with the left wiper to remove his shirt sleeve. The shirt ripped, and he went down in front of the bus. As soon as his feet touched the ground, he started running.

There was a camper at the intersection turning right. He thought that he could make it. Looking over his shoulder, the woman and man exited the bus. The woman raised her arm. He saw a white handkerchief that was placed over the gun to hide it from view. He knew that he didn't have much time. People were blocking the camper. He believed there was still time.

The woman pressed on the trigger. She was so focused on her target that she missed the next scene unfolding. Sawyer looked to his right. Barreling down on him was a second bus. He saw the bulging eyes of the driver as he tried to break. The bus hit Sawyer but the bullet hit a second earlier in the back of his neck.

The woman groaned because she wasted a bullet. The man and woman decided to exit the scene.

The bus continued to roll forward and hit an old man taking his wife out to buy groceries and that car hit another car. Their grocery coupons flew out the window. The bus collected more vehicles along with Sawyer's body before it came to an abrupt halt hitting a tree. The cars bent and buckled in the way things do when mass meets foreign anything. Sawyer was instantly dead. The others were alive. The damaged bus stopped finally, hugging the large oak tree.

The storm cloud released its quick torrent of water making everyone else in the area run for cover. The weather man was wrong. There wasn't anything mini about the rain burst that dropped in the area. The yellow caution flag went up at the race track and then the red flag. The cars were parked on the pit road until the shower cleared.

Trent Rudy later disappeared having watched the accident unfold from his spot across the street. He also recognized the couple on the bus from Big Bear Lake. His statuesque posture and starring eyes made Tracker turn to look at the man. The couple recognized Rudy as well. Trent Rudy was now their new problem. Rudy saw the woman throw the handkerchief away and raise her gun in his direction. He quickly ducked into a moving mass of cars and trucks, disappearing in the rain. He was safe for now.

The rain washed the blood spatter off the bus and the cracked windshield. The red flow from Sawyer's body streamed away from the tree, mixing with the dirty water in rivulets. The liquids went into the gutter pooling with the rest of the mess. All witnesses left the scene. Sawyer laid under the tree, a crumpled mess with wet coupons covering his astonished face. One of the coupons read, three cents off/turkey gizzards. The coupon was an error. The correct coupon was thirty cents off. The error wouldn't matter to anyone. There was nothing left but a broken bag of bones for an undertaker to examine at the end of his day.

There were no more tomorrows for the evil one who killed his brother and his rich ex-wife. He hadn't stayed alive to see if Mic or Dan would live. Vengeance, greed, and revenge were emotions silenced by a second bus and bullet. It was an easier kill for Tracker than she planned which left her unhappy. She needed a challenge to satisfy her killer desires.

The police arrived and contacted Derek. They found the strange collection of lug nuts in Sawyer's pockets, noticed his race manufacturing representative outfit, and read the badge which didn't match his identification card. The police knew that the dead body matched the bad man's picture. They all carried the wanted photo in their pockets. The police caught the man a little too late.

Derek quickly called the manufacturing sponsor and ran to the garage to check the lug nuts. There were two different types of lug nuts in the same name box. Derek had to presume that one of the boxes was defective. He talked to the head pit crew manager who examined the boxes. They believed some of the strange lug nuts were already in the pit area. Both Mic and Dan's sponsors were alerted. The two drivers were alerted. They didn't know how long the other lugs would hold or if they were even on the two cars.

Mic heard the transmission and swore. He didn't want to give up the race. His sponsor let him decide. Mic didn't want to see a black flag. He thought about Tiare and drove back to the pit area. He would lose precious time and be behind a lap, but he didn't want to run the risk of tires falling off. There was always another race and time to be a powerhouse.

Dan decided to remain for two more laps and saw Mic in the pit area. He knew the risk was too much. He remembered the drone and bullet. Dan rolled the race car into his pit crew. The chase was the game, and winning was the goal, but Dan felt good to be alive. Both men moved down in the race standings.

But then there occurred a wreck on the track which caught half the field of cars. One car bumped into another and caused the vehicle to tailspin 180 degrees which slammed the next car into it, rolling the first car's hood so that it peeled back like an orange, exposing the engine with all its smoke. This further created confusion and visibility problems for the other cars. A big cushion was required to avoid being ensnared in the wreck area.

Mic and Dan watched the whole thing unfold. In the end the third car ended up on someone's roof. The drivers hated getting involved in the middle. The metal damage would be high. All the drivers were safe once the momentum stopped. They exited their vehicles when the wrecker trucks arrived and waved to their fans. It was all they could do. Some of the cars wouldn't start again and had to be towed off the track. There were a lot of cars that would join Mic and Dan in the lower race standings that day.

After the race, Derek and Jim informed both men that Sawyer was dead. They congratulated each other on the back. The vengeful, maniac con artist and murderer was gone from their life. They didn't care who wiped him out permanently. They thought he was a waste of a human being a long time ago.

Dan asked, "Were the Showmen announcers talking about you and Tiare?"

Mic grinned and responded, "Yes."

"Congratulations, man. I really mean it."

"Good, because Tiare wants you to be a groomsman at our wedding. She asked me to check with you on the subject except I've been dragging my feet. I was too stubborn to ask you because I wasn't sure where we stood exactly. We were just beginning to be good friends again."

"Thanks, I'd like that very much, good friend."

Mic nodded and left the area to meet Tiare.

Dan grinned, because that meant he would see one of the other beautiful Miami women again. He really liked her from the Miami party. He could use a little ecstasy in his life. He didn't care too much about the lower standing in the race. He was in one piece and Sawyer wasn't. His life would be normal again. Anyway, as normal as it could be considering his career. Dan felt relief. This was the first time in a long time of renewed energy. His future looked bright.

38   Politician's House

RICH JUST LEFT his girlfriend, Melissa. He found some papers that he needed to work on for tomorrow. He thought he heard a short blip from his security alarm and glanced at his computer. There was nothing showing on the device, so he continued with his reports. Suddenly, he thought he saw a glimpse of something or someone pass by the doorway to his den. He went out of the room to investigate and saw the door to his vault was open. Rich hadn't been in his vault this morning. Curious, he stepped inside and felt a slight prick on his neck before going down.

A week passed after the race and Derek was called to the politician's house. He brought Rhonda and Jim with him to investigate. The firemen were watching the house to make sure all the flames were out. The embers were too hot to enter the premises, but the body was moved out of the metal vault. The man's body was being taken to the coroner's office for an autopsy.

Derek approached the police and fireman. The fireman told them that he thought the house had been deliberately torched close to the vault. Most of the house was still standing but the politician was dead. The vault door was locked with him inside. The inside release showed sawed marks and wouldn't have worked. The police knew they were looking at another possible murder case with Rich Madden being the victim.

The story in the newspapers was huge and showed a weeping fiancée urging anyone to come forward if they saw anything. The politician died from a toxic overdose of poison. The Snake woman read the article, and she ordered Max to bring the tracker and friend to Russia. The Snake woman didn't give authorization for the hit. She also saw a picture from a friend with the London police. It was her Tracker near the restaurant where Rich Madden ate. The shot was the picture Jess took.

In the picture, Snake woman saw the car parked to the side and the arm of a man. His left hand was on the window frame. Snake woman zoomed the picture closer. The man was adjusting his mirror. She saw Matin Domingo's gold snake ring with the hashtag marks. She knew the man, Henri, who wore the stolen ring was her Tracker's friend. Snake woman now knew who murdered her old love in the Miami prison with her poison. It was her young cousin, the Tracker. Henri was able to get into the prison undetected. They did the hit against someone she cared about. She didn't authorize their game. She knew that her cousin was out of control.

The Snake woman hired a company to cut a small and large hole in the lake on her property saying it was for a fishing party she was having. Max knew something was up with her because she would only let him know that he must make their arrangements to move to Ireland. She sent Max off in their truck with her family's bedroom furniture and the baby items. He was to attend to their affairs and she would handle her visit with Tracker and her friend. Max took their baby with him and would find a nanny in Ireland for them. He would write up the exchange of the second truck for a private plane for her. She would follow to Ireland later having ended her visit with their two guests.

XXXXX

Trent Rudy saw the article about the death of Sawyer and the politician. He put two and two together. He fingered Derek's business card which was burning a hole in his pocket. He knew that he could give the police his description of the two suspects at large for the Big Bear Lake murders, Sawyer, and possibly the politician.

There was an old photo stuck in the yellow sports car door. The black and white photo was at his old garage. There was a slot in his metal desk drawer where he put the photo. Rudy would go back to his old garage to ask the new owner if he could check the desk. He remembered the photo. In the picture was a woman with possibly red hair with the politician.

Rudy thought he saw the same woman at Big Bear Lake when the squirrel died. She wore a disguise, except the shape of her face seemed the same. In the photo, the woman held a glass jar. It looked like a small snake inside. He couldn't be sure. Was the politician involved in any of the stolen cars or was he only involved with the woman? Rudy wanted out of the whole mess, but the tracker woman and her man were incredibly good at being a killing machine. He thought no one could bring Sawyer down. Yet, the woman and her friend brought about his end in a big hurry. Sawyer was evil and deserved it for killing his brother and ex-wife.

He wasn't sure how the politician came into play except he felt it had something to do with the dead wife. The dead wife somehow owned a yellow sports car. Did the politician buy the car for the broad or was the yellow car a gift from a girlfriend to him? The car was later stolen. Obviously, the yellow car was the bad luck.

Rudy would take another two weeks before he found the courage to call Derek Wright, the Los Angeles investigator. Then he stood for a long time outside his office before finally entering the building.

39   Tracker and Friend in Russia

SNAKE WOMAN WELCOMED her cousin and male friend, apologizing that they would have an opportunity to meet Max later. He was off attending to some business. She moved her few things into Max's bedroom. The rest of the house looked like they had made it their home. All traces of the laboratory were gone and all the baby items.

She cooked large steaks with potatoes and opened a good bottle of wine. She recommended they go into town for some bait. They could go ice fishing in the morning and take the snowmobiles. She told them that it would be fun. They could celebrate with a fish fry to congratulate them on capturing Sawyer. She was pleased about those findings.

Snake woman handed them their final release document and a cashier's check. "You are officially done working for me. Max and I will resign and retire."

The Snake woman looked directly at her cousin. "Isn't this what you have wanted all these years, Theresa, darling? You have wanted to control the business and now you can."

Tracker woman smiled and squeezed her friend, Henri Clan's hand. "It is what I have always wanted, and I'm glad you remembered my name. You rarely use it. Now that I will be in control, please use my name."

"Good, then let's get to bed. We can make an early morning fishing run, *Theresa and Henri*. I've got some fried egg sandwiches and potato sausages in the refrigerator we can take with us in a thermal box and dark coffee in the morning. It will be a fun picnic. There are even moose on this property. I'll take the ropes and gun just in case we see one. Then you can really experience the wilderness."

Tracker and her friend were excited. She loved potato sausage and the thrill of bringing down a moose would be interesting.

Before going to bed, the Snake woman read her files from Max. He was in Germany and located the priest. Snake woman pulled up the photos found in the recycle bin on a computer. She saw her Theresa Tracker with a man in a pose next to a yellow sports car. She saw the contents of the jar. There were other photos of her Tracker with the same man in Miami standing next to a law firm building. The man's arms were touching the woman's sheer slacks in her rear end. The pose was seductive and provocative.

"The lover politician."

The control of Snake woman's business would be wasted on the cousin. The images changed her plans for the cousin and her boyfriend. The morning would be the end of her poison-for-hire business and much more. There were other ventures more prosperous.

The next morning, the three people drove the machines out to the fishing hole site and surveyed the area. The snow covered the lake. The thin ice was waiting. She pointed where the fishing hole had been dug. There were orange marker flags on the holes. They were close. The two guests assumed the marker flags were separate holes. They didn't know it was one large hole and a small one.

"No moose. The timing is wrong. It's probably too early. Let's eat first and then we can fish for an hour. We probably shouldn't stay too long outside in the cold."

Snake woman handed each one their thermos and packaged breakfast.

She saw a moose in the distance after an hour. "It is not your time, my friend. You get to live, and they don't. She put the bodies on the snowmobiles and tied them together. Then she secured the bodies to the snowmobiles with dissolvable tape. She removed their identification papers and started the lead machine, guiding it toward the soft ice in the middle of the lake. Snake woman jammed her sticks with larger rubber bands to hold down the throttles. The machines inched forward slowly moving straight toward the center of the flagged area. The weight started the cracking. The moose looked up and ran away to safety. The machines easily slipped through the thin ice and into the freezing water. The weight of bodies and machines gracefully poured through the water hitting the deep bottom and coming to a rest. The weather changed and started to lightly snow. She threw the rifle into the water. The ice would entomb them. She wore her special gloves and they would be disposed of properly.

The Snake woman knew they wouldn't find the bodies until spring after she was long gone. She climbed aboard her snowmobile to go back to the house to burn all their papers. She placed their clothing on hangars in her room. A special folder of photos was left behind. The police will believe they have caught the killer of the Burrows and the politician. Maybe they will think the body is their snake woman. She hoped they would.

She called Max and made the mistake of telling him what she had done. Max couldn't believe she killed family. "But why?"

Snake woman told him, "She made mistakes and lied to me. She lied about Matin and her ex-lover, the politician. You saw the photo with the yellow car and the jar. How dare she do that pose? The Tracker let the police investigator's wife take her picture in LA. She disobeyed my orders. She was a loose end and I had to clean up. Who else knows about her and us? Where did she put Matin's money? Half was missing. I don't believe the money wasn't on the Burrows. We found out the truth in time. It wouldn't take the police long to get the same results. There's no forgiveness or recovery from her errors. Nothing can correct the wrong. Her death was my call to remove her from her toys, misjudgment, money, and the rest of the world."

Max looked at their small daughter and became worried. "Children make mistakes."

"Theresa wasn't a child. She loved to kill too much."

Max was concerned. True madness had overtaken the woman. He couldn't let his daughter grow up with her in Ireland. Her mind contained no forgiveness for family. He thought he was considered family. She could just as easily kill him or their daughter. Rumblings shook his heart. The little child needed protection. Max would protect her. He didn't need Snake woman anymore. Any type of love for her died in one second. There was nothing but frozen tundra between them. Max would have to fake his love until he devised his plan. The plan to move was good in that there was currently distance between them. In the morning, he would leave Germany and return with their daughter to Ireland to find a nanny. A nanny was all that was required in his future world. He would stay away from women.

The scales were tipping. Stealing a child never works.

40   Woman's Plane in Ireland

THE SNAKE WOMAN decided to have some of the more expensive furniture sold and the entire complex as well. A new, private account was set up. She wiped everything down with bleach. Early in the morning, she drove to the small airfield and made her transaction with the manager. The next day, she called Max to let him know her estimated arrival time. The weather looked clear for flying.

She saw the coastline approaching in the distance. Her neck was stiff from the long flight. She felt the engine hesitate. She looked in alarm at her fuel gage. "How can it be that close to empty? All my calculations are correct. I never fail at this." She quickly scanned the coastline for a place to land. The area was mostly sheer cliffs. "Perhaps a water landing would work, but where?"

Snake woman saw the spot and descended toward the cove. Escaping the plane that was slowly submerging, she thought about her fuel line and made herself look at its location. There was a small hole in the tube; the hole was a cut. Instantly, she realized what happened.

"Max, how dare you?" She was furious.

Swimming to shore, she walked in the early evening light to a small tavern and ordered a corned beef sandwich and beer. No one paid any attention to the woman who wore an old coat and hat she stole from a local farmer. She also stole his hunting knife from the holster on the wall and would be using it shortly. Snake woman stashed her bag of poison and put a slower-acting syringe in her pocket.

She walked the last five miles. She knew he would be up awaiting news of the small airplane that crashed. The fact that there wasn't a body wouldn't worry Max, because the ocean could have taken a floating object a distance down shore. She would have time to complete her mission.

Snake woman was always good at waiting. She hid in the small barn in the hay mow and watched him leave in the truck. She saw the horse and the motorbike. She would give the horse enough food and water for two days and take the motorbike. The truck was too noticeable. She held her new identification card. This would be easy. The nanny left in the evening.

On a whim, she followed the nanny. She didn't know why. The woman was less than five feet tall and seemed to be overweight. It was hard to tell from her heavy wool garments.

They were approaching an older white-washed house that looked like someone added four additions onto it making the house seem disproportionately ugly against the stark landscape. There were amazingly beautiful bare trees and bushes that dotted the trail to the nanny's house. There was no smoke coming from the chimney. She assumed no one was home.

Snake woman noticed the small garden. One of the additions looked strange like it was a greenhouse of some sort. The windows were grimy, but she thought she saw some small trees inside when a small piece of lightning hit. A few large raindrops fell. The nanny was a gardener? She wondered what she grew in there.

"Do you think the woman was growing pot? No, she didn't look the type."

Snake woman hid behind a large grove of trees. The rain drops were getting larger. The nanny turned back as if she heard something. Her grey scarf slipped from her mouse-brown hair. Snake woman fingered her syringe. The nanny was the ugliest woman she ever saw. She reminded her of an alligator in a ditch north of Orlando, Florida.

"What are you doing, Max, with this woman? Normally, your tastes edge toward beautiful. Guess this was the closest person available for the job of taking care of our daughter."

The anger she felt toward Max removed all their years together. There would be swiftness. Nothing would stop the flow of evil thoughts in Snake woman's brain. It ruled her every thought for now. She turned and went back to Max's cottage.

She opened the small refrigerator door and was glad Max had not yet returned. She saw the tube of liverwurst from the butcher shop. The label read one pound and there was a quarter of the nasty stuff left. Snake woman pulled out the syringe and inserted the needle into the meat. It was the appropriate thing for her to do.

Next, she checked on her daughter. The baby was sleeping.

"Still, the nanny shouldn't have left her all alone."

She knew that it was time to return to her hidden spot and wait some more. She watched from the crack in the siding to make sure Max returned. She would recheck things in the morning and give the poison time to work. Snake woman couldn't let his mistake pass. She would have to get herself a new man someday or keep her desires under control if she was going to truly raise her daughter.

The next morning, she heard whistling and looked out to see Max getting water from the old well. She heard the nanny approach. Her crunching old boots on the gravel driveway were a dead giveaway. The poison hadn't worked. Max was still alive. The nanny and Max were in conversation.

"Max didn't eat the liverwurst." Snake woman would need to wait and rethink a new plan. She left the old barn and found her bag of poison stash and grabbed a heavy, fast dose syringe and fondled the knife. She stopped and put a second syringe in her pocket just for her protection.

"Killing Max turned a little harder to accomplish."

There wasn't much time. He would become suspicious if her body wasn't found soon. The sea usually gave up its dead.

The clock showed noon and the nanny left Max's cottage.

"Why is she leaving my baby so soon? Max must be coming shortly." She waited ten minutes. There was no Max. Snake woman snuck into the cottage and opened the refrigerator.

"The liverwurst was gone."

She checked the garbage can and saw there was no paper wrapper. It dawned on her what possibly happened. She needed to follow the nanny once more. She ran. As she was approaching the old woman, the nanny skipped and danced a little bit. Then the nanny bent down, holding out a tiny bite of liverwurst to two white geese from the refrigerator package.

"Oh, no!" said Snake woman. She yelled. "Don't feed the geese that meat or they will surely get ill. They should only eat grains."

The nanny was surprised to see someone. She turned and grinned. Then she popped the small bit of liverwurst in her mouth and swallowed. Suddenly, she teeter-tottered and fell. Snake woman grabbed the meat package and let the old woman fall backward into the soft pond mud. The geese went flying and squawking as far away from the two women that they could get. They knew when to run.

Snake woman approached and saw that the nanny wasn't dead. The spot of meat didn't contain much of the poison.

"You have been lucky today."

No one was around. She could drag the nanny's body into the pond. The body would drift to the other side pushed by the wind. The location was a small town and it would probably take their local doctor a little while to figure out how the nanny died. Snake woman only needed a little more time. This required a change in her plans.

Taking a branch, she scraped the muddy area to remove her footprints. She took the package of liverwurst over to some large boulders and buried the package.

Coming back to the woman lying in the pond, she noticed again the woman's heavy clothes. The temperature was warmer today, but the rain presented a problem. She could leave the old woman or help her. There still was Max Lewis to deal with. Her indecision was costing her time.

Snake woman saw the decrepit wheelbarrow by the greenhouse and quickly deposited the woman in the bucket. She took her to the house and propped her in the chair.

"At least you won't drown or freeze to death."

The house was silent. There was no one there except the two women. She walked into the living room and lit the wood in the fireplace with a long match. Snake woman stopped. There was a vase of dried looking lilies on the table. A memory flickered across her brain. She shook her head.

Taking the flowers, she threw them in the fire. She didn't know why she did what she did.

"The blooms are dead."

Emptying the water in the kitchen sink, she wiped the vase with a cloth to make sure no fingerprints were left.

41   Rudy with Derek

RUDY TOLD DEREK all that he knew about Sawyer, his brother, and Sawyer's ex-wife. He felt either Sawyer did the hits or arranged them through the copycat snake people named Burrows. Then he told him that Sawyer was at Big Bear Lake as was Tracker and her man. Derek showed Rudy pictures and he choose the photograph Jess had taken of the woman. He knew nothing else other than the bus accident and murder that he also witnessed.

Derek talked to him about the Snake woman and why the police were looking for her at the same time. The police believed the tracker person may be a relative or someone extremely close to the leader. The woman may even look similar, but older.

Rudy thought back to all his contacts that he knew throughout the years and looked at the woman again. "Can your person make her hair really dark for me?"

The sketch artist manipulated the file. "Now for some reason, that woman looks familiar, but I can't say for sure. If she does exist, could I still be in danger?"

"Now that information, we do not know. We do, however, believe she has access to all the Tracker's files. The tracker may have taken pictures of you. The other question might arise? What if you have, by accident, met or seen the Snake woman. What if she recognizes you? Or she might connect you to Sawyer who dealt with the copycat snake people. If it was me, I would definitely still lay low."

"But that's what I was doing from Sawyer. I hid out in Santa Monica after he tried to kill me. Then I see him in Santa Monica. It was my bad luck happening all over again. Can't the police protect me?"

Derek looked at Rudy who hadn't exactly been very helpful in the beginning, nor provided them with new information. He could, however, identify the Tracker and her friend.

"The police can help for some time, but then what usually happens is the files become cold and they back off. The Snake woman is very good at waiting and seems to have access to our networks. She is the ultimate con artist."

Rudy swallowed. He was going to move somewhere else. It might be a good idea to forget about police protection. Some of them might be in on the Snake woman's game. Rudy knew how the bad guys worked and the various departments and levels. He was a con artist and part of their underground world. He wanted out of it. That was his only reason for talking with Derek. Rudy fingered the black and white photograph in his pocket of the politician and woman in the yellow sports car. He would hold onto the image and only play his ace card when he absolutely needed it.

Derek also wanted out of the game or at least, an end to it.

"We can get you a new identity and provide you housing and a new job to help you get on your feet, but that is it.

"Okay, I'll take it." Rudy didn't have much money and needed help. Maybe he could get back into the car business. "How about a mechanic's job? It's all that I know."

Derek felt sorry for the man. He also thought Rudy knew something important that could help the police. He was still too scared to think clearly. "Yes, we can do that for you. If you think of anything, let me know."

Rudy got up and sat down. "There was a man and woman that I saw one time at a party in Miami. The name on the outside of the hotel ballroom said, Matin Domingo Party. The woman looked like the Tracker, only with dark hair. She was with a big guy, over six feet five inches tall and he was possibly from Hong Kong. I lived a year in Hong Kong, so I should know."

Derek smiled. He found another connection. "Can you work with our sketch artist for a picture of this man? We have an image of the Tracker friend."

"Sure, he was not hard to forget. The guy even scared me from where I was standing. I stopped looking at him when he noticed that I was staring at his face."

After Rudy left with the information Derek provided him for his police contact, Derek went over to his credenza. He buzzed his secretary to come into his office. She was surprised to see him pouring out the fresh batch of coffee. He handed her the printed files from the sketch artist to distribute to his people and his superiors.

"This case will be interesting in the future to see what comes through our system. I'm going home shortly to my beautiful wife. Please call the florist for me and I'll pick the flowers up on my way home."

His secretary peeked at the photos and smiled. "I'll do that right away."

42 Tiare and Mic's Wedding

MIC WAS NERVOUS, and he wasn't sure just why. He had done the marriage thing before. He looked at his five groomsmen and the bridesmaids. They were waiting at the white flowered altar with a friend of the Wright's who would officiate the ceremony. There were a sea of chairs and people dressed in their finery and waiting in very large white tents. There were three huge tents to accommodate everyone and the food. The party was at a warehouse lot close to one of Derek's very secure and private warehouses. The bride would arrive via helicopter.

He heard a flourish and looked down the red carpeted strip. She hadn't wanted a white carpet. She wanted to stand out when he saw her. His friend, Terrance, played the wedding march with a Polynesian twist. Then Mic saw her with Derek. He felt better now.

Tiare came closer and he saw her white and pearl gown with free floating fabric flowers. Her hair was partially up to hold her pearl and white phalaenopsis orchid headdress with feathers. She had a sheer cape with more sheer flowers that trailed behind her. Tiare's eyes sparkled with a gorgeous mask of eye shadow color. She carried a fake gold scepter. She looked like a Polynesian princess.

"Correction, you look like my Polynesian princess." Mic took her scepter and handed the object to his groomsman, Dan. Dan dropped the scepter and had to pick it up.

Tiare smiled, "Good, because I packed my tow rope in case I need to climb any balconies."

Mic couldn't help but smile. He helped move her cape, so she could stand under the flower arch. They said their vows and Mic felt like he won the best powerhouse race of his life. Nothing would match the thrill of Tiare. She was the one person he could count on to save him. He knew that she loved him immensely.

After the ceremony, they turned and greeted their guests. Mic kissed Tiare and then everyone partied.

There was massive food, wine, champagne, and decorations. The white cake with pineapple filling was another huge design of layers and layers of fondant and flowers. Later, they flew via private jet to a Polynesian island. Only a few close friends knew which one. Their life together would be a good one, because the Wrights' crony families were now massive in size. There would always be a party to celebrate something.

Mic added some pearls to his motorhome paint design and her name alongside with his which pleased her when they came back from their honeymoon. They went house shopping in Los Angeles and Miami. Plus, Mic bought his own race car and was happy. He didn't know Tiare had money and was surprised when she suggested the car for her wedding present to him.

She bought him a different helmet with no stripe for Dan to watch on the tracks. Dan was good at following Mic anyway. They, too, developed their own rhythm on the raceway. A year later, Dan would marry into the Miami crony family. They would join on one team together and remain good friends.

43 Russia and Big Bear Lake

IN THE SPRING, the new owners and their land of the former Snake woman's compound in Russia would be swarming with police after a man and woman's body surfaced in the lake. They would find the snowmobiles and rifle at the bottom of the lake.

A report would come across Derek's desk to show that their identities matched the possible murderers in California. There was little information on the couple and no identification papers. Derek acknowledged that the two people met a bad end. There was a mild dose of poison in the bodies and they drowned.

The new owners remembered a folder left on the premises when they first arrived at their home. Derek clicked open the folder's contents on his computer. He wasn't surprised to see the Tracker woman with the now dead politician. Here was a final connection. The Tracker was one of the man's many ex-lovers. They possibly met in Germany. Derek bet the yellow sports car serial numbers were swapped out a long time ago at Minnow Surf's chop-shop. The sports car looked to be the same make and model. Derek could relate to the hateful look the Tracker wore in one of Jess's pictures. Derek speculated the Tracker probably killed him and not Snake woman. Derek didn't believe the dead body was Snake woman's. He and Jess agreed that she was still alive. Derek was waiting for additional retesting. He believed the dead woman in the lake was the Tracker.

Jess felt the same way. They both agreed the woman was extremely dangerous for anyone to walk across her path. She was unpredictable. Bodies piled up around her. They thought she would hide out in another remote place and use her money which they knew was hidden in many off-shore accounts. Her intelligence and many skills would enable her. She would run free, able to create another business.

Trent Rudy was found dead three months after the tall man was found dead in Ireland. Rudy drowned in a fishing boat accident at Big Bear Lake. There was nothing found in his pockets. Derek wondered why the man went back there.

He sent his man, Brandon Keller to investigate the rental homes and cabins in the area, looking for any woman who looked like their drawing. Derek might as well have sent Brandon to the moon. The tracks were cold. Snake woman was gone or was never there.

The real culprits in the drowning materialized later. They were possibly two speed boats who raced the area. One of the speed boat owners admitting hitting something. An aluminum boat was submerged after their race. He wondered why there was no one in the aluminum boat.

Derek hoped, however, Snake woman stayed out of his country and left the area. He was unsure if her power play with people was over. Snake woman went after the bad guys in a different way. He had to give her credit for cleaning up the territory a little bit, stepping on those who copied or disobeyed her. Anyway, that is what they assumed happened.

Derek thought about the politician and his powerful legal family that still lived in Miami. They owned enough money and could find her. The person who killed their beloved son was Snake woman's apprentice. They didn't care that their son was not a good person. Family was family, but this was a powerhouse one with massive connections. Their connections may be stronger than hers if fueled by a high need for revenge. The next storm could be more destructive. Someone must pay for Rich Madden's death.

No one knew if the scales balanced, other than life became calm again. Evil was laying low for now. The heavy fear and undercurrents dissipated. The edginess was lulled into everyday happenings. His team was glad to go back to the average criminal and con artist, handling burglaries, missing people, and cheaters. There were no serial killers running around the Los Angeles area with their crazy ideology.

California was a desirable place to live, especially when the sun came out. Families thronged to the ocean and its sandy beaches. They were looking for a piece of paradise. The current and closest Polynesian island was a familiar place.

"Catalina Island." Derek called his Captain to stock the boat.

44   Jess and Derek

PLEASURE WAS HAPPENING. They were taking the yacht to Catalina Island where War Julio and his family were already moored in his motorboat. They picked up Jim and Mary Beth earlier. Their children would have a blast together. Derek was pleased the families would have a relaxing time. Jess told him their plans for barbeque. She bought paper and helium pineapple balloons for the children to release when the sun set.

Their chef created a volcano surprise for dessert. Derek worried a little bit about that word. His young daughters were learning how things blew up. They talked to him about the volcano when he visited with them. Jess told him that he was being silly. He shouldn't worry. The volcano had nothing to do with the cottage she owned a long time ago. Her blast was fueled by propane. Their volcano was white cake with strawberry and pineapple crème that oozed out of the top with gravity and some help.

"Did I scare you a little with the volcano?" asked Jess.

"You always scare me; but come here, I do need a kiss." Derek pulled her into his arms. This was where he wanted to be ever since he met the strange girl fascinated by diamonds and a specific diamond heirloom. He thought he would never catch her heart or find a lost heirloom. She was constantly ahead of him.

"Did you know Mic and Tiare have decided to rent an apartment at Rhonda and Skid's building?"

"That is great news, because we should see more of them."

"Yes, and their friends, Terrance and Michelle Reston, have also moved into the building. Mic is working on an album with the Terelle Triumphs during the off-race season."

"Now, I like that idea. The album should be pure entertainment."

Jess laughed, "Yes, and they will be off-season when we have our next party to honor Dean Crain."

"That's perfect timing, honey. I believe I already know the theme. It's either racing or islands."

"Yes, maybe we can use both concepts, or we might do a San Francisco theme."

Derek blew out his breath. His wife never stopped. He loved it. He was going to have to hang on for another ride.

"San Francisco sounds excellent. We could buy a pier."

Jess stopped.

"No, no, I'm kidding."

Derek looked worried. The chef announced that they were ready to leave the pier.

"Are you ready?"

Jess hugged her husband. "I'm ready and stop worrying."

She brought a ceramic, hand-designed volcano style holder made for each of them for the adult's treat. The oysters laid around the rim in their own butter sauce and didn't blow up. After she heated them in the microwave a little, she did have two sparkly red streamers that neatly fit in the top hole. She tried to get the chef to make some bread dough flames except he refused to color his dough with an ugly red, purple, or green. He told her bread must look like bread and not some king cake from New Orleans.

Jess told her chef that he did have a point. The bread dough flames would be a good story to tell Derek. There are some things a person shouldn't change. She planned for their private evening with small homemade bread loaves with red and black pepper on the top. The chef would arrange the bread on long oriental chopsticks to add an island feel. The champagne wrapped in green palm fronds would be waiting. She showed Derek the champagne opener in her closed hand.

Derek laughed. "Oh, yeah."

"I'm glad we are good." Jess was happy.

"Most definitely, wonderfully good." Derek was going to enjoy the little party. Their yacht lifted a little, headed straight west, and then turned. They were cruising to their island.

XXXXXX

A year would go by before a call from the police in Williamsburg, Virginia, would interest Derek. A woman lived there in a very large estate. The neighbors contacted the police due to the construction activity. The police took some time before they went to the home. There was no one home or no one answered the door. The police let the incident drop.

However, the neighbors called again about some speedboat the woman's workers used. They didn't like the noise. The police went back to the house and argued with one of her workers. That's when the police began checking out the woman's background.

The woman took vacations to perfume companies and several lotion distributors. In viewing her passport, she traveled all over Europe. Countries she visited were Spain, Germany, Italy, Greece, London, and Ireland. There was a problem with her entry stamp in Ireland. The mark was blurry.

The Virginia police checked with Ireland. They reviewed documents in their system, and the woman didn't show up as a person entering their country, only exiting. They wanted to question her regarding those facts. Derek would read the date she left the country. The closeness in likeness of Max Lewis and the dead Max Reafer would make Derek take notice. He contacted the Virginia police who were awaiting a search warrant. Derek wanted to be with the police when they searched the woman's house.

The coincidences piled up to create an unreal scene. There would be an opportunity to cross paths with a resilient, possible psycho.

More Exciting Books
in A Wright Series
by Author

Linda McKown

Diamonds Blondes and Poison – Book 1

Dead On Coordinates – Book 2

Wild Golden Obsession – Book 3

No Easy Target – Book 4